The Acquittal & Other Stories by AM Burrage

Alfred McLelland Burrage was born in Hillingdon, Middlesex on 1st July, 1889. His father and uncle were both writers, primarily of boy's fiction, and by age 16 AM Burrage had joined them. The young man had ambitions to write for the adult market too. The money was better and so was his writing.

From 1890 to 1914, prior to the mainstream appeal of cinema and radio the printed word, mainly in magazines, was the foremost mass entertainment. AM Burrage quickly became a master of the market publishing his stories regularly across a number of publications.

By the start of the Great War Burrage was well established but in 1916 he was conscripted to fight on the Western Front. He continued to write during these years documenting his experiences in the classic book War is War by Ex-Private X.

For the remainder of his life Burrage was rarely printed in book form but continued to write and be published on a prodigious scale in magazines and newspapers. In this volume we concentrate on his supernatural stories which are, by common consent, some of the best ever written. Succinct yet full of character each reveals a twist and a flavour that is unsettling.....sometimes menacing....always disturbing.

There are many other volumes available in this series together with a number of audiobooks. All are available from iTunes, Amazon and other fine digital stores.

Table Of Contents

The Acquittal

They kept Frenchal waiting below-stairs a long time—a very long time. Evidently the jury was not finding it easy to make up its individual minds. It must have been three hours before the ten men and the two women were brought back, closely guarded by those ridiculous javelin men, and ranged in neat rows in the little tiered box on the right of the judge's throne.

It had been a long trial, interesting enough to the newspaper students of such matters, who have only the tit-bits served up for their delectation by expert journalists; but those compelled to be in court, and the sensation-seekers, who had come for entertainment, had found long periods barren of drama and even of interest.

It was a poison trial. John Frenchal stood indicted for the wilful murder of his wife by administering arsenic. The evidence was all circumstantial and almost entirely technical. Two pathologists with conflicting opinions had each spent hours in the witness-box and given evidence which counsel, jury, and probably even the judge, had failed wholly to understand. The summing-up had been neither for nor against the prisoner, and the scales were evenly balanced when the judge said his last words to the jury. Only the newspapermen, highly experienced in such matters, knew during those long three hours what the verdict must eventually be. 'Oh, of course, he did it. But they haven't quite brought it home. The jury are bound to funk it. They'll have to let him off.'

Frenchal sat and sweated. He had no means of telling whether this long deliberation of the jury was in his favour or against him. He had borne himself all through the long trial with a calmness and dignity which had compelled a certain amount of admiration. Now, when at last they tapped him on the shoulder, he wondered if he would be able to walk.

Yet, once he was upon his legs, strength and the power of emotion returned to him, and he walked firmly up the wooden stairs between the two warders. He had scarcely reached the rail of the dock when a door opened on the other side of the court, and all around him sounded the rustling and scuffling of people rising from their seats. Through a mist he saw the judge in scarlet and ermine seating himself on the throne under the Royal arms; very far away, it seemed, he heard voices. The members of the jury were answering to their names. Well, one way or another, it would all be over in a few seconds now.

'Members of the jury, are you agreed? Do you find the prisoner at the bar Guilty of wilful murder or Not Guilty?'

'Not Guilty.'

He wondered for one aching moment if he had heard aright, if that short first word had really been uttered. Then one or two sentimental women, high up in the gallery on his left, began to clap and were sharply reprimanded.

What was happening now? The judge was speaking to him. He saw a faintly cynical smile on the thin, hard lips. Then a finger touched his arm and a voice whispered: 'Come along, sir. Better come downstairs and wait a bit.'

Inherent courtesy made him bow to the judge. Then he turned and walked downstairs in almost a state of trance. He did not need the supporting hands on his arms. He was strong enough, but nothing just then seemed real.

The warders, who had been sternly respectful, were now more friendly. But there was something cynical and restrained in their manner, as if they thought him a lucky man, as if they knew! They brought him brandy which brought new life to him and gave his surroundings more of the deeper colours of reality. He lit a cigarette and handed his case to the two men in blue, each of whom selected a cigarette and put it in his pocket. His counsel came down to congratulate him and receive his thanks, so did his solicitor, who had worked wondrously hard. But on the faces of each of them he remarked that smile, a little like the judge's, a little like the warders'—as if they thought him undeservedly fortunate.

Presently he remembered that now, after long weeks of confinement, he was free. He got up and spoke of going. His solicitor bade him wait a moment, and went to confer with a policeman standing near the door.

'Better wait a little while. You're not in a hurry. There's a crowd outside. Presently there'll be a rumour that you've been smuggled out, and then they'll go.'

A crowd! That meant a crowd which might possibly be hostile. So they thought he did it, did they? Well, confound them, they were right. Everybody knew, except those twelve fools who, faced with a responsibility beyond their powers of endurance, had given him the benefit of the doubt. The prosecution had bungled its work badly; he could have told that harsh-voiced, eminent K.C. where he had got the poison and how it had been administered.

The policeman came forward.

'Your car's just been round to the back, sir. I sent it away and told the man to come back in about twenty minutes.'

'My car?'

'A taxi, sir. He said it'd been ordered.'

Frenchal turned to his solicitor. 'Did you order me a car?'

'No. I was going to, of course.'

Then who had? Some friend of his who was present in court, he supposed. But he had seen no friends. Even Edith—but, of course, it would have been too much for Edith. And the train of thought, starting on a new trail, ran on. Did Edith know? Thank heaven that something hadn't come out at the trial. If the fools who, as the defence triumphantly proclaimed, could find no adequate motive, had known about Edith and put her in the witness-box, the trial might have come to a different end. Edith's circumspection, the secrecy on which she had insisted through their intrigue, her slavish worship of the conventions, and the outward show of respectability which had helped bring about the crime, had at least saved him from the consequences. This handsome young widow, his neighbour and his wife's friend, had not been mentioned at the trial.

The tale was as old as passion and crime, the yearning for romance of an unscrupulous man, who, tied to a wife who bored and irritated him, felt the sands of his youth already beginning to slip away. If Edith Longley, who came to live in the grey house across the common, had loved him a little more and her own reputation a little less, the affair might have ended less tragically in some other court.

Frenchal was in the forties, and he had been married for nearly twenty years to a woman who had begun to bore him on their honeymoon. He was not capable of giving a love which outlived passion. His wife was; and she was sentimental and clinging rather than ardent. He soon came to hate her. He had hated her for years, and it was her relentlessly continuing to love him which had lit an ugly red fire in the ashes of boredom and indifference. If she'd only been indifferent, too, if she'd only left him alone instead of fawning around him and making his flesh creep with her caresses and endearments! Like a great ugly cat, she was, he thought, purring and nudging against him for caresses! Her little attentions to his comfort, and she was forever warming his slippers and filling his pipe, sickened him because they spoke of her unwanted love. He had borne it wonderfully, he told himself, and might have gone on bearing it indefinitely if the whisper had not come that life—as he counted it—with its ardours and capacities, was draining away. And then had come Edith Longley, young and warm-blooded and widowed, to bring him once more the thing he called love.

Oh, yes, she loved him—in her fashion. But she would not burn her boats. She did not like to think of certain houses being closed against her, and of having to find new friends among people who were not quite—you know! If he were free as she was it would, of course, have been so different! No more of the simple and ugly story need be told.

The courthouse stood among narrow streets in the older part of a cathedral city. It was at a few minutes to six on a damp, dark autumn evening when Frenchal stepped out quickly and quietly through an arched doorway and into the taxi-cab which awaited him. He had troubled in fastening the door, and the driver, perhaps because he was anxious to get a view of his fare, left his seat and came round to help him.

'Farnham House, Benford Common,' said Frenchal.

'Yes, I know, sir.' As if everybody in the county didn't know his address by now!

'Wait a moment. Who ordered you?'

'A lady, sir.'

'Oh, really! I wonder who. Tall, dark lady with black hair?'

He was describing Edith Longley. The man shook his head.

'No, sir. She was fairly tall for a lady, but from what I could see of 'er 'air it was fair and goin' a bit grey. I didn't notice what 'er clothes was like. They wasn't any particular colour.'

'Thank you. All right.'

Who could it have been? Not Edith, certainly. It was more like—hang it all, it might have served for a description of Mary—Mary dead and in her last resting place. What a strange spark that fellow's words had struck, half ghastly and half humorous. If one believed in ghosts! Faithful and affectionate wife arranges for the comfort of her husband after his trial for having murdered her. Just what Mary might be expected to do if she could! She had always tried to live up to copybook maxims on the subject of forgiveness and returning good for evil.

It was a whimsical thought, but it began to give him discomfort, and he tossed it away. Not that he believed in anything of that sort. He held that dead men and women were as dead as dead dogs. Nor had his conscience given him the least trouble. All he had endured since his arrest was an agony of anxiety regarding his own fate. That anxiety was past now, and into its vacant place came crowding a host of other and smaller cares. His financial condition was a worry. He had been compelled to spend on his defence much more than he could afford. And Edith? How would Edith feel towards him now, when he came back with the stigma of his trial. For he was well aware that he had no more proved his innocence than had the prosecution succeeded in proving his guilt. And—hang it!—who was that woman who'd ordered the car for him immediately after the trial? Hair beginning to turn grey, clothes not any particular colour . . . Just like Mary; you never noticed her clothes. Why couldn't he get that silly bizarre thought out of his head? He began to sweat again and felt weak.

The car swung out into a broad, lighted thoroughfare and turned south. Frenchal tapped at the glass in front of him and spoke through the tube. 'Drive straight on until six o'clock,' he said, 'and then stop at the first inn. I want a drink.'

Six o'clock found them on a lonely stretch of road, but within a minute or two the lights of Camcross village shone mistily at them out of a hollow, and the driver slowed down and pulled up before an inn which stood a little way back from the road on the outskirts of the hamlet.

Frenchal got out and took a step or two towards the door, only to discover suddenly that he had a shrinking fear of being recognised, and needed the moral support of the driver.

'You'd better come in and have something,' he said.

The driver followed him. They entered a brightly-lit tap-room where some half a dozen rustic workers were already assembled. One or two of them made way for Frenchal before the narrow counter, on the other side of which a fat, florid landlord stood polishing glasses.

'A large Three Star brandy,' Frenchal muttered, 'and—what's yours?—oh, and a pint.'

The landlord brought the drinks, and stood for a moment trying to look over the heads of his customers and then craning his neck to right and left.

'Well, that's a rum 'un,' he said. 'Wasn't there a lady come in with you?'

Frenchal started and spilled some of the spirit.

'No,' he said, and almost snarled the word.

'Well, I could 'ave sworn I see a lady follow you in.'

'I thought I see one, too,' remarked an aged farm-labourer from a far corner. 'Must have been shadders.'

The landlord laughed uneasily, and delivered himself of the inevitable joke.

'Well, you and I 'ad better take more worter with it, George, 'adn't us?

You ain't got an evenin' paper on you, I s'pose, sir?' he added, addressing Frenchal.

'No.'

'Ah! I wanted to know 'ow the trial of that there Frenchal's gettin' on. You don't 'appen to know if it's over?'

'Yes, it's all over.' Frenchal tried to speak indifferently. 'He got off.'

There was a low, growling chorus and then a laugh.

'There, 'Arry!' said a voice. 'Wot did I tell yer?'

'I don't care wot you told me,' the landlord retorted hotly. 'I reckon they didn't ought to 'ang nobody after that!'

'You'd 'ave liked the job of 'anging 'im yerself, 'Arry,' chuckled the old labourer in the corner.

' 'Anging 'im! I'd like to burn 'im! Tres this 'ere Sir James Champion to defend 'im. Bin a pore man, 'e'd 'ave swung all right. All I've got to say is, if 'e didn't do it, nobody did.'

Frenchal had the wit to perceive that he had not been recognised. His identity was known only to the embarrassed driver, who shuffled beside him awkwardly, sipping his beer. So this was how the Man in the Street regarded him. Well, it was more or less what he had expected. He braced himself, knowing that the driver would have a tale to tell before closing-time that night.

'Possibly,' he said coldly, 'if you'd attended the trial you might have come to another decision, the same as the jury. After all, my friend, you've only read bits of it in the newspapers.'

'I've read quite enough, sir, and nothing won't alter my opinions. You mark my words, there was a lady in that case which nobody knows nothing about. 'Ushed up, somehow, that was. Bin a pore man, now'.

In spite of himself, Frenchal was put out of countenance. A lady in the case! Strange how a stupid, vulgar mind, which did not know how to begin to reason, had stumbled upon the truth! He turned to the driver, trying to smile.

'You ready?' he asked. 'Goodnight, landlord.'

He wanted to snarl an insult at that fool of a publican, and yet felt that he might be grateful for the warning. How closely the eyes of his little village world would watch him now! If he married again too soon, if he saw too much of Edith, the self-appointed critics would draw their own conclusions.

He cursed them in thought as he clambered into the car. Let them think and say what they liked; prove what they liked now. Not again could he be tried for his life because of Mary. And yet he knew in his heart that popular opinion mattered much to him, that he could not bear social ostracism.

During his time of waiting he had dreamed of a popular acquittal, of people coming out to cheer him as he drove back to his home. He knew already how this dream was to be fulfilled. People knew! He was returning to them, not stainless, but having the benefit of a shadowy doubt.

If only he could get away! But financial ruin already stared him in the face. He had been living beyond his income for years: and the price of his defence had added very materially to the encumbrance on his small property. To sell now would leave him poor indeed. He saw himself tied fast to his little house, the 'gentleman's farm', with its memories of Mary and its circle of hostile neighbours.

Nobody except the driver saw his arrival home. The car purred up the short drive, turned in the circle of gravel, and stopped outside his door. He saw a light in the dining-room and the flicker of a fire on the blind. They expected him then!

He got out and tipped the man, handsomely. The man thanked him hoarsely, and shame-facedly wished him luck. 'He don't look like a murderer,' the driver thought, forgetting that no murderer ever did. His indoor servants, a married couple named Townsend, both came to welcome him. The door opened as he set foot on the steps, and revealed them standing in the lighted hall. They were both obviously embarrassed, and had spent long hours in discussing how they should receive him if, and when, he returned. They were agreed that it was unnecessary to make any speech of congratulation, and yet they could scarcely behave as if nothing had happened. Their both being in the hall to receive him was a tacit vote of confidence, for they were both loyal believers in his innocence. How could he be a murderer when they had been with him so long and knew him so well?

Frenchal was a little cheered and reassured by the sight of them standing there, with the shy, tremulous smiles on their old faces. Like them, he found it unnecessary to refer to the ordeal through which he had just passed, but he shook hands with them in turn.

'Well, Townsend, how are things?' he asked, trying to assume a bluff heartiness of manner.

'Pretty much as usual, sir. Dick Baines is comin' up early tomorrow mornin' to see you about the stock. Dinner's all ready for you, sir, and Mrs T have done the chops the way you like 'em.'

'Dinner ready! How did you know -'

'We was rung up. sir, just before six, and told as you'd be home about seven.'

Frenchal frowned, and, because he was bewildered, his over-strained nerves snapped the thin thread of his temper.

'But hang it, I didn't know that myself, then. The—the—it wasn't over until after five. Who rang you up?'

'A lady, sir. She just said that you'd be in for dinner at about seven. Nothing more than that. And then, of course, sir, we knew'

'What lady was it?'

'I don't know, sir,' Townsend faltered. 'It gave me rather a turn. I thought it sounded like'

'Hush, T!' his wife interposed sharply.

She might have added that she, too, had received a 'turn', when her husband had rushed to her white-faced and said that the voice he had just heard on the 'phone was so like the old Missus's that he didn't know how to hold the receiver to his ear.

A chill struck Frenchal, accompanied by a sudden spell of giddiness. He knew exactly what Townsend had been about to say, and found himself not daring to ask the man to end the interrupted sentence.

'Oh, somebody who knew me, I expect,' he said, with a quaver in his voice. 'We shall find out tomorrow, I dare say. Did you say dinner was ready, Mrs Townsend? All right, I shall be ready, too, in a couple of minutes. I'm just going up to wash.'

He went upstairs to his dressing-room, where a fire, blazing in the little grate, gave him a welcome with which he would have gladly dispensed. The sight of that fire burning there reminded him of Mary. A fire in his dressing-room was one of Mary's little 'attentions', which used to irritate him because they proclaimed her unwanted love. For such he was expected to kiss her and say, 'Thank you, darling!' A wave of anger swept over him. What right had Mrs Townsend to light fires without orders? He was a very poor man now; he must make sweeping economies.

He was halfway to the linen cupboard in search of a towel when he glanced back at the hearth and uttered an ugly little choked cry. Just inside the fender were his slippers and pyjamas, and nobody but Mary had ever dreamed of laying them there. Seeing them there made him think that after all she couldn't be dead, that she was in the next room on the other side of that half-open door, preparing for dinner. He who believed in nothing but the plain creed of materialism glanced stealthily and uneasily at that door, and involuntarily his ears listened for once familiar sounds—footfalls, the rhythmic sound of long hair being brushed, the tinker of hairpins in a china tray.

He went downstairs again, stumbling and cursing. In the kitchen he found Mrs Townsend and rated her wildly. What the devil had she meant by lighting that fire? He couldn't afford fires in his dressing-room. And what the devil did she mean by putting out his pyjamas and slippers like that? When he wanted a valet he'd engage one, he told her.

Mrs Townsend looked startled and abashed.

'I lit the fire because I thought you'd like it, sir,' she said. 'You often used to have a fire. And I'm sure I didn't touch your pyjamas and slippers, sir! No, that I didn't!'

He turned to Townsend, who had come in time to overhear.

'Then it was you,' he said.

'No, sir. I haven't been upstairs all this evening!'

Frenchal included the pair in a snarl.

'Well, one of you must have done. One of you is lying. I found them there!'

He turned away muttering, trying to shut out from his mind the dreadful thought which now clamoured all the more insistently. Suppose neither of them had put his shoes and pyjamas there to warm? Suppose they had been put there by the same woman who had rung the Townsends up on the telephone and sent the taxi round to the Court House at Hanchester. Suppose it were true, after all, that people had souls which survived their bodies? Suppose Mary still hovered about him, unseen by him as yet, forgiving him for what he had done, still anxious for his comfort, still loving him and angling for his love in the ways which had irritated and nauseated him while she lived?

He grappled with the thought and flung it away. It was too fantastic, too utterly appalling. He told himself that his brain must have been affected to create a fancy so hideous, so utterly unfit for any man's mind. But thoughts, once begotten, bred quickly, and their dreadful freakish offspring over-ran him.

He found himself unwilling to go up to the dressing-room again, and dispensed with washing. Instead, he passed through the gloomy hall into the dining-room. The hall was only dimly lighted, and for him the great, shapeless blots of shadow were the lurking places of other shadows. Now that he had begun to imagine things he could feel Mary's presence. She was watching him sorrowfully, hungrily, always somewhere behind him, and cunningly eluding his gaze whenever he gave way to his sick fancy and swung about, staring this way and that.

The dining-room was more cheerful. It was brightly lit up, and a fire burned cheerfully in a wide, old-fashioned grate. A place was laid for him at the end of the table where he had always sat. Here there was little at first to remind him of Mary, but he noticed, as he was about to sit down, the empty chair at the opposite end. He got up and pushed it back against the wall. He was a sick man, he told himself, his nervous system had been deranged by what he had already endured, and his fancy was likely to play him tricks. Suppose he looked up suddenly at table and saw in that opposite chair No, he dared not think of it!

With Mary's chair out of its accustomed place he was satisfied for a moment or two. Then, with a curse, he realised that this slight rearrangement of the furniture would not escape the notice of the Townsends. They might even divine the motive which had made him move it, and begin to suspect, and whisper that the master was haunted by his conscience. So he returned the chair to its old place, found himself weak and perspiring, and went to the sideboard for brandy. As he helped himself liberally he was conscious of a Presence which was aware of his misery—although, perhaps, not comprehending the cause—and was nauseatingly sympathetic and trying to caress him.

He thought, quite reasonably, that he was going mad. Never in his cell had he been tormented like this. There he had faced another terror in single combat. He made a supreme effort to reason with himself as he drank the spirit and felt a little of his courage ebbing back. Very soon he would find out who had ordered that taxi for him and rung up the Townsends. All these sick fancies had sprung from the fact that some good-natured busybody had tried to befriend him. And, of course, one of the Townsends had put his slippers and pyjamas in front of the fire upstairs, and afterwards forgotten all about it. They were a pair of fools, and the sooner he got rid of them, the better.

He began to be angry with that perverse imagination of his. If it had to whisper to him that Mary was near him, why couldn't it have been logical and told him that she hated him and wished him dead. He could have endured the imagined presence of a vengeful spirit, but not the spirit of Mary, forgiving and smarmily loving as she had always been. And suppose his imagination went further, learned new tricks? There was no knowing where it was going to stop.

Sooner or later he would have to go to bed, to sleep in that dressing-room which led into another room where, lying in the double bed, she used to come in and say goodnight, bending over him and brushing his face with her long, loose hair. She had never plaited it, and sometimes, after she had washed it, it was dank and sticky. Suppose he were to fancy - Ugh! It did not bear thinking about!

Mrs Townsend brought him in soup, and then a brace of chops. He ate little, and was careful never to raise his eyes to that chair at the other end of the table. He drank unsparingly, keeping to brandy, but it seemed to have no more effect on him than water. Only when one of the Townsends was in the room did he look straight and calmly at that chair at the far end of the table. Townsend came in after the plates had been removed.

'Some letters for you, sir,' he said apologetically, I'm sorry. I forgot them.'

He took the little bundle and turned the envelopes one by one until he came to one addressed to him in a thick, round, feminine hand. As the door closed he tore it open feverishly, and stared out of hot, dry, feverish eyes at Edith's unsigned note.

In the event of your being acquitted, please do not make any attempt to see me. I wish neither to see you nor speak to you again.'

So Edith knew! He realised now that all the time she, of all people, must have known. And this was how she now felt towards him—she for whose sake he had risked everything. He stared at the written words in an agony of frustration, of foiled desire. His heart seemed to rise and swell as if it would choke him. Then terror had him by the throat and he stood rigid in an agony of fear.

High up near the right shoulder he felt on his arm the sympathetic pressure of slim fingers. Somebody, some woman standing behind him, was touching him, fondling him, being sorry for him. It seemed to his stricken senses that the air close to his ear was faintly stirred by a fluttering warmth of breath. This—this was no fancy. She had touched him like this a score of times when he was angry, when things had gone wrong, when he was disappointed and unhappy.

He could not move nor cry out. He knew that she was there, that, could he turn his head, he would endure the culminating horror of seeing the presence which he already felt. She was being sorry for him, 'smarming' him, because his poor heart had been bruised by her rival! He suffered physical besides mental nausea. He stood there in indescribable agony of mind, while his life and reason rocked and reeled on the edge of some fathomless abyss.

At last the hand on his arm relaxed its pressure. He felt himself being softly patted twice. Then he reeled to the sideboard, clutched it, buried his face in his arms and crouched there, moaning.

He had at last to face the dreadful prospect of going to bed, and although he drugged himself with all that was left of the brandy, he walked upstairs as sober as any living man.

The fire in the dressing-room was nearly out, but there was still a glow in the ashes, and he thought of trying to revive it. But a fire sets shadows in motion all about the room, and he could not face the prospect of a wakeful night in such a company. He undressed, with his gaze for ever turning sidelong to the door which led into the room which had once been Mary's. The electric light switch was by the door, and he kept the light burning when he got into bed. Then it seemed to him, as his courage revived a little, that he might have some chance of sleeping if he turned it out. Besides, in the dark, one might feel and hear; but at least one could not see, and all the man's five senses had become his enemies.

In the dark he returned to bed, thankful for the closed door between him and that other room. But he was hardly in bed for the second time when it opened with the click of a slipping latch, setting his heart jumping and his nerves tingling.

He remembered that this was an old trick of that particular door, and wished that he had remembered to find the key and lock it. He could hardly endure the thought of it standing a few inches ajar, but to get up and close it—no, he could not quite do that. He began to sweat again at the thought of all manner of hideous possibilities which began to jostle like gamins to attract his attention.

For a full hour he lay tossing and turning, hearing the bed creak under him at every turn. It was a noisy spring mattress, and when Mary was alive she always knew when he was wakeful and often came in to ask why he could not sleep. That thought instantly begot another which was unspeakably hideous. He wished he hadn't remembered. He plunged over from his left to his right side, as if to shake himself free of it. The bed creaked—and an answering creak from the bed in the next room brought the sweat from every pore in his body.

He had heard that sound before when Mary was awake. He used to lie still then, lest she should come in to him with her tender inquiries and her irritating nerve-destroying solicitude; but never did he lie as still as he lay now.

Frenchal, rigid as a corpse, scarcely dared to breathe. His pyjamas, sodden with perspiration, clung to him and irritated his skin. He found himself in an attitude quite unendurable, but dared not stir. When at last he moved, it was as if his tortured nerves had rebelled and shifted a leg and elbow. The tell-tale bed creaked, and sharp upon the sound he heard an answering creak from the bed on the other side of the wall.

He was quickly losing control now, and a low moan escaped him, and it was answered by a familiar sound in the next room—the soft, shuddery sound of somebody turning over in bed. Sparks of light now began to dance before the man's eyes, keeping time with the galloping of his heart. He stuffed bedclothes into his mouth and bit into sheet and blanket. He writhed this way and that, and the tell-tale mattress creaked and tinkled.

In the next room a pair of feet thudded softly on the carpet beside the double bed. Footfalls came softly to the door. The hinges creaked, and the footfalls crossed the threshold. The window fronting Frenchal's bed was a dimly luminous rectangle. For a moment it framed part of a human shape which moved, looming nearer. He closed his eyes. He was far gone now, and capable of no other movement. He heard the sound of breathing drawing nearer, and then, close above him, the soft, dreadful voice he knew so well.

'Can't my darling sleep? Oh, what's the matter with my darling?'

And there fell upon his upturned grimacing face a soft rain of cold, damp tresses.

When Mrs Townsend brought Frenchal's morning tea at eight o'clock, she knocked without being able to make him hear. Presently she walked in and pulled up the blind. Then she turned, looked at the bed, and uttered scream after scream, which brought her husband to her side.

It was a doctor who, speaking in low tones to others in the room, presently drew down the blind again.

The Green Bungalow

Foul deeds will rise,
Though all the earth o'erwhelm them, to men's eyes.

When Freeceland arranged nearly to have a nervous breakdown and so acquire medical backing for a month's rest in the middle of the winter he overlooked the fact that his Chief might exhibit some curiosity as to where he was going.

Freeceland had a Government appointment; he was assistant vice-something or other in a Government office, and sick leave was easy enough to obtain. He had, however, to make some decent pretensions to being ill, and the medical certificate he laid before his Chief might have led one to suspect that he was not long for this world. He must have complete rest and complete quiet in some extremely bracing place. Freeceland admitted that he had thought of Brighton.

'Brighton,' said the Chief, 'is not quiet, nor is it bracing. The Hove end is even relaxing. I'll lend you my bungalow at Reed Bay.'

'It's awfully good of you,' said the wretched Freeceland, whose mind had been running in the direction of golf and occasional theatres.

'Reed Bay,' continued the Chief, 'is just the place for you. It's bracing; there's an east wind enough to cut your head off this time of the year. It's quiet enough, too, in the summer. This time of the year one might describe it as God-forsaken. There are no amusements, of course, and there isn't any golf; but then you couldn't play golf if there was. Hardly anybody lives on the beach this time of the year, so you won't be worried by neighbours, and it's miles away from anywhere. My dear fellow, it's the very place for you.'

Almost before he knew it Freeceland had allowed himself to be bullied into accepting the loan of the Green Bungalow. He returned home in a state of mind that it were kindest to call 'dissatisfied', and his wife and his wife's sister prepared regretfully to accompany him. I looked in upon them after dinner that night and announced my intention of coming, too, adding that I was not so inhuman as to allow them to go into exile without a fourth for auction-bridge.

The real reason was that Doris Dreever lived in one of the bungalows, and her people, partly from an eccentric love of the place and partly from economy, remained there during the winter. I had met Doris there the previous summer.

I cheered the Freecelands up a little by telling them about the Dreevers.

Then Freeceland exclaimed:

'Oh, by Jove! and we shall see something of Hartley. He's got a cottage on the Downs, about a mile inland.'

'It won't be so much like exile after all,' said I. 'Who's Hartley?'

'A very good chap, but a bit of a recluse, and no wonder. He's had a rotten time. No harm in telling you, since all the world knows it. About twelve years ago he was tried for murder.'

'Really? And acquitted, I suppose?'

'Yes,' said Freeceland, 'but acquitted in such a way that a lot of people cut him. He didn't prove himself innocent, but the Crown hadn't quite enough evidence to hang him. If it had been anything less than murder he'd have been convicted, and convicted wrongfully. When you meet him you'll agree with me that he couldn't hurt a fly.'

'That sort of thing,' said I, 'is enough to sour any man.'

'I feel sorry for him already,' said Gertrude Freeceland. 'I shall be glad to meet him.'

Next day I wrote to the Dreevers, sending the keys of the Green Bungalow, telling them more or less what was going to happen, and begging them to engage an efficient charwoman. Thus when four days later we went down to Reed Bay we found fires lit and tea awaiting us.

Directly after tea I went round to the Dreevers, and brought Doris back with me to supper. In the ordinary way, I suppose, the Dreevers should have waited two or three days and paid a twenty-minutes' call; but there is no such thing as convention on the beach.

The front door of the bungalow opened straight into a sitting-room—a cross between a dining-room and a morning-room. Opposite was a door leading into the dining-room, and to left and right were other doors leading respectively to the kitchen and a bedroom, for the bungalow, being only of one storey, and intended to accommodate a number, was inclined to be rambling.

Doris and the Freecelands—who immediately showed symptoms of liking each other—and I had just settled ourselves comfortably around the fire when a curious thing happened.

The dining-room wall shook violently as if something struggled against it. A loud, metallic clang sounded on the wall close to the roof. Then the latch clicked, and the door, which opened into the room where we were sitting, was violently flung open.

'Oh, come in!' cried Gertrude Freeceland, laughing.

Freeceland jumped up. 'That's deuced odd!' he said.

It was. I was sitting nearest the door with my back to it, and as it flew open I had an impression that reminded me of a certain black day in the Ypres salient, just before I received the wounds which got me my discharge from the Army. I had not heard the coming of the shell that burst beside me in the mud, but for the fraction of a second I had a queer feeling of something heavy hurtling down on me. As that door flew open felt it again, and flinched. 'Nerves,' one would say; and 'nerves' I was willing to believe it then.

Freeceland pushed past me and gazed into the next room.

'Nothing there,' he said.

'Wonder what it was,' cried Julia, his sister-in-law, who wore, like the rest of us, rather a startled look.

'Wind!' said Freeceland. 'You can't expect a place like this, with hardly any foundations, and built entirely of timber, to behave itself like a brick house. Still, it made me jump for the moment.'

Apparently our nerves were, for some reason or other, a little unstrung.

Shell-shock had left me particularly susceptible to sudden noises, and the others seemed quite as disturbed. Later we all jumped again, and I opened the door and looked in to discover that the new disturbance was occasioned by the charwoman who was gravely laying supper.

When at last we were summoned in for the meal I made a discovery which had eluded me at tea.

'Why,' I exclaimed, 'this room is an old railway-carriage.'

Gertrude laughed.

'Hadn't you noticed that before?' she exclaimed. 'And a first-class compartment too. Look at the ceiling.'

I looked up and saw that it was arched, and covered with rather dirty, cream-coloured lincrusta, such as is used to cover the ceilings of some first-class railway-coaches.

It was not so strange that I had not noticed it before. Furniture and decorations had wrought miracles of alteration. The long row's of windows were completely covered by green curtains. Above them was a shelf lined with books. A curtain reaching to the floor entirely concealed the door. But between the shelf and the windows the communication chain still remained, and it was hanging down in a loose coil as if it had recently been pulled.

'Funny!' said Freeceland. 'I could have sworn the chain wasn't hanging down like that at teatime.'

'That,' suggested Doris, 'is what we must have heard rattle against the top of the partition. It must have slipped down.'

I rose and pulled it up again. Then I jerked it down, and it took quite a perceptible effort on my part.

'Don't see how this thing could slip,' said I.

I went to the door and pulled aside the curtain. It was very obviously the door of a railway-coach. There, in faded black numerals, just below the window, was the number 6787.

There was no need to tell any of the others that I felt uncomfortable about the room, and the fact that it had once been a railway-coach made me still more uneasy. My nerves were far from sound, and I tried to put down my sensations to their vagaries. I had never before accounted myself a superstitious man, but I could not help wondering if that particular coach had any special history. It was not difficult to account for noises, or even for the sudden opening of the door, but I did not see why that chain, which was so rusty that it was difficult to pull down through its narrow grooves, should drop of its own accord.

It had dropped, however, and it continued to drop. If we pulled it up at night we found it down in the morning; also the door of the room was always open.

We spent the next three or four days in laziness—reading, playing bridge, and taking short walks. I saw Doris as often as I decently could, and Freeceland paid his friend, Hartley, a visit. We exchanged calls with the Dreevers, but Doris, lured by me, came oftener than her people—at least once a day.

On the afternoon of the fourth day I met Doris in the village, and had to decline an invitation to her people's bungalow on the following night.

'You see,' I said, 'a man named Hartley is coming to dinner. It wouldn't matter so much if I wasn't there when anybody else came, but I don't want it to look as if I don't want to meet the man.'

I told her what I knew of Hartley's history, and Doris, who knew him by sight, nodded agreement with me.

'It's terribly hard luck on him,' she said. 'I must say he doesn't look like a murderer.'

'What does a murderer look like?' I asked her mischievously.

Doris did not know; she was only positive that Mr Hartley did not look like one, and that was good enough. I took her back with me to tea at the bungalow where Gertrude and Julia were alone, Freeceland having taken the train into the nearest large town with the intention of begging, borrowing, or stealing one or more bottles of whisky.

After tea, which was served in the front room, I led Doris through the railway-coach dining-room into the beach-garden beyond.

It is hardly necessary that I should intrude my personal affairs into this story, but it would be as well to mention that on our return I was not in a condition of mind to pay much attention to Gertrude and Julia. Doris had said 'Perhaps' several times in answer to my questions, and finally 'Yes'.

When at last we returned I was rather less observant than a bat. I did, however, notice, in a subconscious sort of way, that something seemed rather wrong with Julia and very wrong with Gertrude.

Well, man is a selfish animal and I did not pay much heed to them. Doris having consented to take me and mine, including the piece of shrapnel that had yet to work its way out of my back, I took little interest in anyone else's affairs. We said nothing to them about ours, and Doris refused to stay for supper, having, I suppose, something to think about.

I saw her home, and returned to be pounced upon by Gertrude.

Freeceland had not yet come back.

'John,' she cried, 'don't for heaven's sake laugh at me, but this place is haunted.'

I myself had fancied something of the same kind, but never dared to put it into words. Gertrude's doing so gave me a queer shock.

'John knows,' said Julia, 'I could see he knew.'

'There is,' I admitted, 'something queer about the place, but'

'There are no "buts",' Gertrude interrupted. 'Don't let's be afraid of giving things their names. The bungalow is haunted.'

I sat down.

'Well,' said I, 'don't tell Vicky (Freeceland). His nerves are a bit wonky, you know.'

'Vicky knows, only he won't admit even to himself that he knows. He's that kind.'

I lit a pipe. 'What's been happening now?' I asked as soon as it was going. 'Any more noises?'

'I've seen something,' Gertrude said quietly but impressively. 'When you and Doris went into the garden I thought you were in the next room. We stopped here because we didn't want to—er—to interrupt you.'

Gertrude paused and smiled wanly. All unstrung as she was then she was still capable of a certain archness.

'Presently we both heard a noise in the next room like two people struggling and banging against the wall. I thought you two were squabbling over something in fun. I've seen you handle that poor girl as if you were both playing Rugby football, and looked in to remind you that there was glass behind those curtains. The room was dark, and—well, two people were there struggling—two men. They were very shadowy and indistinct, but I saw them for a moment, and then somehow I seemed to lose them.'

'Lose them! How?'

'I don't know. I couldn't see them any more, but they were there. They pressed close against me and past me, gasping and panting, and then—then the door burst open of its own accord. Julia saw that happen.'

I looked at Julia. Clearly she did not doubt one word of her sister's narrative.

'You're quite sure?' I began puffing laboriously.

'You know,' said Gertrude, 'that I am quite sure.'

After that there was nothing more to be said.

Next evening Hartley duly arrived; and just before he came Freeceland said something that set me thinking.

'I say,' he exclaimed, i'd forgotten about the dining-room being an old railway-coach. I hope it won't upset poor Hartley.'

'Why should it?' Julia asked.

'Because the murder of which he was accused took place in one.'

It set me thinking, although I had no right to think. If what naturally occurred to me were true it would be a strange coincidence. Still, all things considered, it would have been strange if I had not wondered a little.

When Hartley came he proved to be a very florid man with glasses, about fifty years of age, I should think, but his fair hair had retained its colour and had scarcely thinned. He somehow gave me the impression of a man who suffered from heart trouble, and just as I came to that conclusion he told us that he did.

The suddenness of the tragedy made it all the more appalling and grotesque. Hartley had scarcely been inside the bungalow five minutes when it happened.

'Whisky's good for the heart,' said Freeceland with a smile, 'I managed to "wangle" two precious bottles yesterday. Come along in and have a spot, you two men.'

He lit a candle and preceded us into the dining-room. I went last and closed the door. Candle in hand, Freeceland marched over to the sideboard, and Hartley looked at him.

Even in that dim, wavering light I saw him change colour.

'Why,' he said, even as I had done, 'this is an old railway-carriage.'

Neither of us made answer, and Hartley smiled rather horribly as if to reassure himself. His hands moved nervously towards his throat.

'I shall be glad of a whisky,' he faltered, 'I'm not—feeling—very fit.'

I think we were both embarrassed. Freeceland was busying himself in getting out the bottle, but I had no such occupation.

'Are the glasses here?' I asked rather fatuously, and drew the curtain aside from the door to grope for the handle, prepatory to going out.

A sort of gasp from Hartley caused me to turn my gaze upon him. His eyes were huge, bulging, horrible. His gaze was directed upon the door at the spot where my moving the curtain had exposed the number—6787.

'My God!' he cried faintly, and almost protestingly, 'my God!'

I can't say precisely what followed.

Somehow the candle went out. Freeceland doesn't think he dropped it or blew it out, but he cannot be sure. Simultaneous with the sudden darkness came the crash of a heavy body falling.

'What's the matter?' I cried out. 'What are you two struggling over?'

'Don't be a fool! We aren't struggling!' said Freeceland's voice, high and agitated. 'Come here, quick!'

But two people were struggling there in the darkness. They brushed against me and past me, locked in a struggle for life or death. The door flew open, apparently of its own accord, and a panel of light from the next room fell across the floor. It showed Hartley lying prone and still, his face yellow and wax-like, and—well, the reverse of peaceful. It never did look peaceful, that face. When I knelt beside him he was quite dead. Heart-failure, of course.

We had the curiosity to go to the British Museum and read in some old newspapers an account of Hartley's trial. He had been accused of murdering a rival in business by half-throttling him in a railway-coach and flinging him out on to the line, thus breaking his neck. The victim had managed to pull the communication chain, but the train stopped too late. The number of the coach was not given, but we are pretty certain that it was 6787.

The Kiss of Hesper

He was scarcely twenty years of age, a short, slight, pale youth, with colourless hair, irregular features, and dull brown eyes. He filled the post of junior clerk in the office of a firm of merchants in a small provincial town.

His salary was a pound a week, upon which he lived and clothed himself.

Speaking broadly, he had no prospects, nothing to look forward to in life. John Malpas was the joy of the office. It required a butt, and he was admirably fitted for that unenviable post. He was not a gentleman, but more fastidious than his office mates. His untidiness, plainness of feature, melancholy bearing, slow, nervous voice, gave those with an aptitude for mimicry plenty of scope for exploiting their talent. Even the office boy laughed at John Malpas behind his back, and was subtly insolent to his face. It was the custom of the head clerk to jest respectfully concerning him with the junior partner, when the latter was in gracious mood. The humour of the rank and file of the office vented itself in sending Malpas on fools' errands, arranging booby traps for his discomfiture, torturing his sensitive soul by inventing scabrous stories about him.

Malpas bore it all in silence. The idea of retaliation never occurred to him. He had never been to school, never played games, never kicked in his life.

His parents were both dead, and he was entirely friendless—as utterly alone as a castaway on some uninhabited island. Very often a desire for companionship, friendship, love sprang up within him, stinging all his blood to madness. But he fought it down with a strength of will which would have seemed incredible to those who knew him. He felt in some vague way that he was a philosopher, but he could not explain his thoughts even to himself.

There were times when he derived a real pleasure from morbid melancholy, and other times when he dared to hope for something to lighten the drab colouring of his life. His one recreation was reading, and in spite of the paucity of his means he had amassed a small library of second-hand volumes. Most of the standard authors and the poets were there. He loved Swinburne, who taught him that 'even the weariest river winds somewhere safe to sea', and Browning, who believed that 'what began best can't end worst'.

He had read the great love stories of the world, idealised by the magic pens of the great masters, and longed intensely, silently, for a great love to enter into his life, even if it passed on after but a day's sojourn, leaving a lifetime of misery in its wake. He had even gone out into the streets to give Fate the opportunity of bringing him into contact with a kindred soul.

Sometimes at night he walked up and down for miles, looking up at the darkened houses and torturing himself with the thought that She, his twin spirit, whom God had created for him, and him only, might be somewhere behind the dingy walls and darkened windows.

The influences of his only friends—his books—had taught Malpas to loathe vulgarity. His correctness of speech was the delight of the office. In the course of an ordinary conversation he brought out long words which surprised and amused his audience, who little guessed that he was quite unaware of anything unusual in his mode of speech. If he were a prig, he was an unconscious one.

Naturally, Malpas's mode of living affected his health. He got scarcely enough to eat, and that of a kind containing little nourishment. He suffered acutely from dyspepsia and palpitation of the heart. Lying at night with his ear to the pillow he could hear pulses throbbing unevenly, stopping at times, while he drew a deep breath and waited in deadly suspense. Sometimes he would suffer from attacks of weakness, and there were other times when breathing was a labour to him. But he never worried about his strength. It was out of the question for him to see a doctor. He paid fifteen shillings out of his pound a week for board and lodging.

On a Saturday afternoon late in the winter John Malpas paced the streets of the little town where he lived and laboured. He was suffering from a headache, which took the shape of a leaden heaviness, rather than a pain, but which was sufficiently vexing to prevent him from enjoying his fireside and his books. Rain had fallen during the morning, and the pavements were greasy with mud which the boots of pedestrians had brought from the roads.

An out-of-date scavenger machine passed up and down the street, its heavy brushes throwing the mud into high banks in either gutter.

Two young men from Malpas's office passed him on their way to a football match. They nudged each other and laughed. Old Malpas was pottering about by himself, as usual!

Malpas saw them, and the ghost of a smile broadened his mouth. After all, he considered, if he could not enjoy football matches, they could not enjoy Meredith. And yet he was aware that they were getting far more out of life than he. They understood each other, and enjoyed each other's companionship; they were good-looking after a vulgar fashion; they passed everywhere as normal young fellows, and doors were open to them because they could converse on trivial subjects, and be amusing after a fashion. And Malpas knew, too, that later on they might be loved by good women, and afterwards by their children; that they would live happily until they gave up their Philistine souls, perfectly content with their mediocrity, rejoicing in the material things of life, desiring nothing better, knowing nothing better.

And he envied them. He could not analyse his mind, but he sickened with everlasting striving after the unobtainable. He had been brought up differently from those who laughed at him. He felt himself superior to them, but deep down in his soul he would have given worlds to be like them.

And later on in the afternoon he passed Watson, the head clerk, who gave him the shortest of nods. Watson was with a girl, and did not know that he should have raised his hat. Nevertheless, Watson was happy in the thought that he was behaving with the utmost courtesy. He was dressed in a style that he would probably have described as 'classy', and he was with a pretty, doll-like girl, whose expression told all and sundry that she thought the world of him. To her he was the gentle knight without reproach, the man who could do no wrong. And he loved her with all the subtle delight of love, yet he would have sneered at sentiment beautifully and delicately expressed.

Malpas was sorry for Watson, while he envied him,. Watson was doomed to enjoy love with a dumb soul and lips that might utter only commonplaces. Malpas pictured his own mind under similar circumstances. It would be a beautiful rose-garden, and each blossom a beautiful thought. In his way he was quite as egotistical as Watson, and nearly as conceited.

Presently Malpas was conscious of a lull in the traffic, and a sudden stillness broken by the slow, solemn hoof-beats of walking horses.

He turned and beheld a funeral procession coming slowly down the street in his direction.

It was a very modest funeral, but what it lacked in splendour it gained in pathos. The undertaker proceeded on foot and in advance, a squat, unshapely figure in ill-fitting black. Behind the sombre countenance, which he had assumed out of regard for business, was an expression of placid self-satisfaction. He was a conspicuous figure, and enjoyed being thus before the eyes of his fellow-men. He seemed blatantly conscious that the occasion was just as good an advertisement as a half-column in the local paper.

Behind him came the hearse, and through its bevelled-glass panels John could see the coffin.

It was a small coffin, little larger than a child's, on which rested two dingy wreaths and a cross of artificial lilies. Behind, at equal distances, came two mourning coaches. The usual crowd of louts and ragged children, who will follow anything from a drunken man to a Salvation Army meeting, followed in the wake of the procession.

John Malpas stood on the edge of the pavement holding his hat between his hands. As the second coach passed he turned and followed it with his eyes, and found himself standing shoulder to shoulder with a man of the small tradesman type. The latter had removed a pair of steel-rimmed spectacles, and was wiping them on the comer of a handkerchief. He glanced round at Malpas, and their eyes met. A certain kindliness in the man's face emboldened Malpas to make an inquiry.

'Who is it?' he asked, glancing after the procession.

'It's a girl,' was the answer. 'A lass of seventeen or so. Hesper Vane. Her father's old Vane, the saddler. Maybe you knew her?'

John Malpas shook his head, and, without answering, lost himself in a wilderness of surmises. Was Hesper pretty? Had she been glad to die, or had her young life been joy-bound? And then he began to think of Browning's Evelyn Hope, who had died at sixteen, but whose soul still belonged to her lover, and would be his through the long ages until the new life should come in the old one's stead.

Then, scarcely knowing why, he began to follow in the wake of the funeral.

It led him through the outskirts of the town, between rows of dingy villas, down a long lane, where the blackbirds and thrushes were beginning to build in the bare hedges, and round the angle of an old church wall, which seemed to need all the support of its heavy buttresses.

The procession drew to a halt before the churchyard gate. Malpas stopped too, and, standing hidden behind the wall, asked himself why he had come. He could hear a few whispered words of command from the undertaker, a shuffling of feet, and presently nothing save the restless jingle of harnesses. It had commenced to drizzle, but he passed into the churchyard with his hat under his arm. A little crowd had gathered in a far comer, mourners, children from the streets, and a curious few, mostly of the female sex, to whom a wedding or a funeral is of much the same interest. A surpliced curate completed the picture.

Malpas approached and mingled with the crowd. He was conscious of many sounds—a restless scraping of feet, an intermittent whispering, and the quiet sobbing of some unseen person; above it all he heard the monotonous Oxford-and-Church-of-England voice of the curate as he read the burial service.

He read it hurriedly in an habitually reverent tone. No doubt he wanted to get home out of the rain, Malpas thought, without accusing him of callousness. He must have buried so many people, poor man, and this was but an incident in his daily life; he was used to burials just as doctors and nurses are used to death and disease. In a few minutes he would take off his surplice and call on Lady Revill in time for tea to try to interest her in the forthcoming bazaar. There was no reason why he should think any more of the frail little body lying beneath the loose earth; there were millions of other girls, and the great heart of the world would go on beating as before.

It was soon over. Malpas heard a shower of earth fall upon the coffin and saw the curate close his book and approach a middle-aged couple in deep mourning, who stood side by side staring glassily at the open grave. Striking figures these, standing there so still and looking so lonely in the crowd.

Malpas walked slowly away, feeling a little ashamed of himself. He should not have been there. He had been drawn there, he thought, by a curiosity that was almost indecent. His brooding melancholy increased into poignant grief, which the lowering sky, the rain, and the sad little scene round the grave could not have accounted for.

Hesper Vane! Had he heard the name before? He must think. Something shadowy and elusive lurked just beyond the horizon of his memory. Was it a face or a name? Was it the wraith of a memory of some childish dream, when he had longed for, and pictured to himself, the sister that never came to him? It awakened a sense which was more than memory, and stretched before the eyes of his soul was a pleasant land of sunshine and trees and tall grass and meadow flowers. He did not know what it meant; he knew there was something lost, something that kept just beyond reach of mind or memory, and hovered without in the garden of shadows.

His brain reeled, and he put the thoughts away from him. But all through the evening the name of the dead girl kept recurring to his mind, and brought with it curious fancies bred by his little stock of books. He took down a much-thumbed volume, and read of a Blessed Damozel who leaned over the Bar of Heaven and watched the progress of the lover she had left on earth. And he read, too, of a man who had loved a maid in some previous existence, and whose soul was doomed to revisit the earth in many bodies and in many lands until he should find her again and the old love lift the curse.

That night he dreamed of Hesper, and, dreaming of her, loved her.

He dreamed that she stood before him stretching out warm, white arms, with love shining in her eyes. Like the Blessed Damozel of Rossetti's imagination, 'Her hair that lay along her back was yellow like ripe com.' He tried to reach her and could not, but the warmth of requited love suffused him, and the dream faded and left him smiling.

At the office on the Monday following, Malpas was even more absent-minded and dreamy than ever. He was soundly rated by the head clerk, but gave scarcely any of his attention to the torrent of stinging sarcasm. He was trying to recall something, battling with a lost or blunted sense. His eyes were striving to see beyond the horizon, and his deaf ears strove in vain to hear the call of forgotten years.

Every Saturday and Sunday for the next two months he visited Hesper's grave. At first it was an unsightly mound of earth, its ugliness intensified by white and withered flowers; but as the year advanced the young grass peeped through, and it was as green as many of the older graves by the time a stone appeared at its head.

Malpas often brought flowers, but they were red flowers, because he loved Hesper. With him her name, or her imagined personality, was an obsession. He did not know by what process of the mind he had formed the conclusion that Hesper was the lost love of some former existence, he only knew that he loved her with an intensity that was purged of all earthly desire.

Every night he met the child-spirit in a misty field of dreams, and they spoke together of bygone days. But when Malpas awoke, Hesper robbed him of his store of memories, and all the day he groped for that which was beyond his reach, and listened for sounds which his ears were untuned to hear.

At the office he fared worse and worse. His fellow-clerks, who had often hinted that he was mad, began to believe what they had said in jest. It was an open secret that John Malpas stood in hourly peril of dismissal.

The year advanced along the well-worn road. The gaunt black hedges began to clothe themselves in green, March sent her booming hurricanes, April her rain, and then May, calling forth the sun, danced light-footed over the land, leaving in her footsteps young buds and blossoms and all the gladness of awakened life.

One hot night, Malpas, unable to sleep, crept out of the dingy little house where he lodged to drink the cooler air of the country. Of late he had been troubled with sudden attacks of giddiness and nausea, pains in the left side, violent palpitations of the heart. He knew that his heart was not strong, and half suspected that it might be diseased, but the thought troubled him little.

The night was fine, and a rising moon tempted Malpas farther than he had meant to go. Half-forgotten fairy tales crept back into his mind, and some of his lost childhood came back to this boy who had grown old so long before his time.

There was something in the air which Malpas felt without being able to analyse. As he walked his face parted long strands of gossamer spun between the hedges, and this brought to his mind some fantastic picture he had seen—all cobwebs and fairies and gnomes, with quaint faces and gnarled limbs.

His feet led him to the churchyard wall, and there he paused for a moment, hesitating before he clambered over. It was the first time he had visited Hesper's grave at night, and a feeling of awe made him tread cautiously and throw quick, nervous glances to right and left.

He found the grave and seated himself on the dewy grass near the foot of the mound. He felt very near to Hesper, and a certain melancholy joy possessed him.

His soul called to hers over the void between the worlds.

The graveyard was silver and black, and as the moon climbed higher up the arch of the sky the silver tide encroached upon the shadows thrown by a clump of shrubs. The air caressed him with a warm gentleness. It seemed that innumerable spirits looked down on him through chinks in the black pall that stretched across the heavens, some smilingly, others sadly, and yet others with fathomless expressions in their solemn eyes. Voices called him, softly, insistently, until the air was full of whispers. Then a sensation that was strong and yet subtle, not fear, and yet akin to it, took hold of his heart. He felt his blood rushing in a full tide to his head. The moonlit scene became a mist of grey-blue, he heard himself exhaling noisily, quickly.

He knew that Hesper, clothed in her earthly form, was close behind him. He turned and saw her.

She was just as he had always imagined her. Her face was moon-white and a delicate oval; her eyes looked wild at first, because they were strangely bright, but as he gazed in them he read kindness, tempered by more than earthly understanding. A long robe of spotless white enveloped her. She sat, leaning towards him, with her chin between two delicate white hands. 'Hesper!' he said. He was surprised at his own calmness. Nothing akin to fear remained in the wave of emotion that surged over him.

She smiled at him very sweetly, and he drew towards her.

'Hesper, I never thought you'd come to me. I dared not even pray for it. But you know what I've been thinking all these months—you must know! You must know how I love you!'

'Yes, I know.' The voice was very clear and musical, and sounded strangely distant. 'That is why I have come to you.'

'You love me!' he cried. 'Hesper!'

He leaned towards her as if to take her into his arms, but she motioned him back with a gesture that he was powerless to disobey.

'Hesper!' he cried, 'mustn't I touch you? Take me away with you—take me, take me! Do you know how bitter the world is?'

She inclined her head.

'I have lived in it. But you must remain a little longer, John. It is hard to be patient, but the reward is great.'

'There is no love as I know it in the world you come from,' he murmured.

Her eyes grew more mysterious. 'You do not understand,' she said.

He held yearning arms towards her, and presently his hands dropped and his fingers began to tear at the root of a daisy.

'My God!' he cried wildly. 'And we missed each other in life. If I had known you, you should not have died. I would have wrestled with Death like Samson, and won you from him. I would have become a Man, I would have taken life between my hands and won a place in the world for both. But I missed you, and I'm a weakling, Hesper. Take me away with you. I hate the world! I have nothing to live for!'

'Be brave,' she said softly. 'Remember that we love each other. Remember that I shall always be near you, although you will not see me. And now I must leave you.'

'You will come again!' he cried.

She did not answer. She was no longer there. He found himself suddenly alone, staring at a crushed daisy plant which he held between his hands. How still the night was.

Every night he came to Hesper's grave, and every night the child-spirit met him there. Perhaps he was mad, and the sweet apparition was only the outcome of a mind distorted by loneliness; but I like to think that it was his loneliness and misery that touched the pity of a holy soul, so that It came back from the City of Promise and made heavenly music on the aching heartstrings of the boy.

The inevitable happened at last, and one afternoon at the office Malpas was told that his services would not be required after the lapse of a month.

It was a blow, although he had expected it for some time; but the thought that he was in danger of losing his bread was less painful than the thought that he might now have to leave the town to seek it.

It might mean an everlasting farewell to Hesper; so that night he came to sob his heart out on her grave.

'Hesper! Hesper!' he cried hoarsely, 'come to me!'

He looked up, and she was there, gazing at him with kind, grave eyes, and her sweet, musical voice asked what troubled him.

He told her between sobs, and she, having listened gravely, offered words of counsel.

'Go out into the world,' she said; 'earn your bread, and seek the love and sympathy of some living woman. Later, when you are old and lonely, you shall think of me once more, and afterwards meet me in the World beyond.'

But he cried: 'Hesper, I can't leave you, I can't, I can't! I hate the world! I hate everything but you!'

She looked at him with a new light in her wonderful eyes.

'Think,' she said; 'is life so hateful to you? Is there nothing in the world to bind you?'

'Nothing!' he cried.

'Then—kiss me—John.'

He scarcely heard the words, but their meaning broke upon him like a longed-for dawn. He uttered a cry of rapture and leaned towards her. His arms enfolded her. His lips bent to hers

Heaven grant that in that moment he tasted all that he had yearned for, that warm arms held him, that warm, red lips pressed against his own.

The sexton found him in the morning lying on Hesper's grave with drops of dew glistening on his clothes. The old man shook him.

He thought at first that John Malpas was only sleeping.

Crookback

Tremlett told us the story around the drawing-room fire one Sunday night. For some reason the half-dozen of us who made up the weekend party had risen above frivolity and entered upon a state of high seriousness, which was very unusual on such occasions. I don't know who gave us the lead. I only know that we drifted from a desultory conversation about the relationship between Spiritualism and the churches into a discussion on Spiritualism itself.

The believers and unbelievers were equally divided, and the argument that ensued was about as heated as the circumstances permitted. Everybody was deadly serious. Such humour as there was had a savour of bitterness. Young Parslow wanted to know how anybody could follow a cult which claimed to produce the miraculous, and only succeeded in satisfying the blindly credulous with a few transparent frauds. What could any man with a sound and logical mind believe, in view of the fact that every medium who had come prominently before the public, had sooner or later been caught in the act of cheating? Sift the evidence, and you found none, unless you took the word of a fraud and a self-deceiver. If the dead could speak to us, he said, we should know all about the next world from the first voice beyond the grave. Surely we thought better of our dead than to suppose they would return and shake tambourines for our amusement at the bidding of some vulgar hireling. What was not vulgar about the proceedings was farcical.

Fie went on to remark that there was no real evidence of continuity.

Occasionally one heard of a ghost story which seemed possible to believe; but nearly always a thorough search yielded an explanation. If it were possible to get a sort of trunk call through to the other world, our dead would surely have something better to tell us than the inane stock phrases which the charlatans kept for their customers.

I saw Mrs Richardson quivering slightly. Her lips were drawn in a tight line. She was one of those women who had outworn many creeds, and now clung tenaciously to the last, as if fearing to be left with nothing. I could feel a tension in the atmosphere, and knew that there would be trouble unless Tremlett interposed.

I glanced across at our host, and found myself meeting his gaze.

'What's your opinion about it?' I asked, before Mrs Richardson could mass her forces for attack.

He shook his head and laughed.

'No, you don't, young man. I decline to be drawn into this. I believe in what I call ghosts, which shows that I have a highly unscientific mind.

Parslow has just been saying that there is an explanation to every ghost story—I suppose he meant a material one—if one searched for it enough. I think I could tell him something which came under my notice, and happened in this very house, which would trouble him to explain away.'

Mrs Richardson was diverted from her intended attack, as I think Tremlett intended she should be. She looked across at him eagerly. Parslow took up the challenge by demanding to hear the story. A desultory chorus from ail of us seconded him.

Tremlett lit a cigarette, and gazed thoughtfully into the fire, I haven't told the story for years,' he said. 'One is liable to be disbelieved or laughed at. However, if you want corroboration my sister Muriel and Arthur Brinkner will tell you the same extraordinary things, although neither of them cares to talk about it.'

Tremlett cleared his throat, and, after a moment's consideration, began the story which I am about to repeat in his own words as faithfully as I can remember them.

We used to come here as children (said Tremlett) when there seemed little chance of our ever inheriting the property. The house belonged to our uncle Wilby, who was really no uncle at all, but a distant connection who liked to consider us as his nephew and niece. He was devoted to children, and used to fill the house with us and our small cousins.

I remember him as a very tall grey-haired man with a very kind face, and a very gentle voice, about the last man in the world you would take for a retired colonel. The most delightful time of the day was always the hour before bedtime, when he would have us children into his study—it's the morning-room now—and tell us stories. The room was always like an oven, for he had been too long in India to keep warm at home without enormous fires, and it smelt deliciously of his cigars. I can see us all now in a half-circle around the fire, gradually creeping farther and farther away from it, and hugging our little roasted legs.

He had a delightful way of telling stories, and his repertoire was long and varied. Nearly always, if one looked for it, there was a moral, although the pill was always too thickly coated with sugar for us to realise it. He had a great horror of cruelty, and he was always driving it into our heads to be kind to each other and to animals.

I suppose he made up most of his stories, for he was clever enough to intrigue our interest by giving them a setting familiar to some or all of us. I wish I could remember in detail a story he told us about this very house. We children used to love the place, partly because it was just the sort of house one used to read about in wildly exciting mystery stories. We thought it was at least a thousand years old, and of course, part of it is pre-Elizabethan.

Muriel has only a hazy recollection of the tale he told us about the poor hunchback youth who was heir to a great property some time in the seventeenth century. His uncle, who was the next heir, had at least one good reason for hating him, and caused the wretched youth to visit him in this very house, after which he was never seen again. I know it reminded us all a little of the Babes in the Wood. I know the exciting part of the story, and incidentally the moral, consisted of the dreadful things that happened to the uncle and all who had a hand in the murder—for, murder it doubtless was, although the assassins were never brought to book. Muriel and I both forgot the story too long for either of us to recapture more than a vague recollection of it.

I was twenty-eight and Muriel was twenty-two when poor uncle Wilby died, and I found myself to be heir to this house and the greater part of his property. I had a clerkship in the Foreign Office at the time, and Muriel was keeping house for me in a small flat off Sloane Square. Arthur Brinkner was then our most frequent visitor, but although we had been friends ever since either of us could remember, I did not flatter myself that he came to see me. Anybody could tell in what direction those two were drifting.

It was late in September when Muriel and I came down here to take up the reins. Mrs Watts, the housekeeper, received us in a most stately manner, and showed us all round the house as if we had never been in it before. She had an enormous bunch of keys, every one of which was labelled, and she took us into every room, expatiating on its merits or its demerits.

I said every room. I meant every room except one. There was a bedroom in the front—the one next to yours, Parslow—which we found locked, and for which she had no key.

'Colonel Wilby was always funny about that room,' she said. It had always been kept locked, and if there were a key to it, it certainly was not in her possession.

I remember Muriel and I were a little amused about it, and even made jokes about poor Uncle Wilby keeping a Bluebeard's chamber. I was indifferent as to whether the room was opened or not, but Muriel said she couldn't endure the thought of living in the same house as a room which she knew nothing about. I daresay feminine curiosity had a great deal to do with it. Anyway, I gave way to her and sent for a locksmith.

If we had expected anything in the nature of a find we were doomed to disappointment, although, except that it had no dressing-room, it was one of the best bedrooms in the house. We found inside a stripped double bed, some heavy old-fashioned furniture, a few early Victorian novels, which seemed to indicate the period when the room was last used, and any quantity of dust.

Nobody seemed to know why the room had been kept locked, and we accepted the most feasible explanation—namely, that the key had been lost, and Uncle Wilby, having already more bedrooms than he required, had never troubled himself about it. Muriel took rather a liking to the room, and as we still had some workmen on the premises she had it redecorated and made it what she called 'Pretty'.

We had been in possession about three weeks before Muriel had the house more or less to her taste; and during those three weeks she had been telling me about five times a day that we ought to ask some people down. I was not in those days a very gregarious animal, and I rather shrank from the idea of a house-warming. Fortunately, I had a safe card to play in resisting Muriel's suggestion.

'Weil have a crowd down later at Christmas time,' I said. 'Meanwhile I'd rather we only had Arthur.'

Muriel's argument against 'only Arthur' was a mere pretence, and Arthur Brinkner duly arrived one Wednesday in the middle of October. It was amusing to watch Muriel playing hostess to him in this new environment. I've put you in the Mystery Room,' she said, as the three of us sat at tea in the hall. 'You won't mind, will you?'

'The Mystery Room?' said Arthur. 'What's that?'

'Oh,' returned Muriel, 'it's a room Uncle Wilby always kept locked, because it's haunted by all sorts of dreadful apparitions, and everybody who sleeps there either goes mad or becomes white-haired in a single night. But I know you're not afraid, Arthur.'

'Being a very courageous man,' he laughed, 'perhaps I shall only go iron-grey.'

'Don't let Muriel fill your head with a lot of nonsense,' I said. 'We found the room locked for the simple reason that the key has been lost. It's like Muriel to invent a ghost story about it. If you don't like the idea of it, there are plenty of other rooms. I don't know why Muriel put you in there.' To this day I believe that Muriel had in the back of her mind some faint suspicion that the room had once been supposed to be haunted, and that she put Arthur into it by way of an experiment. Arthur, as you all know, was a hard-headed brute who had very little fear of anything which was tangible, and still less of anything which was not.

'That's all right,' he said good-humouredly. if I don't like the room, I shan't be afraid to shout.'

As a matter of fact he liked the room very much. It faced south, and got all the sun, and all through that October we had been having glorious weather.

Next morning when he came down to breakfast he found Muriel already at the table, and she greeted him with a laughing, 'Well, Arthur, seen the ghost?'

'Four altogether,' he replied in the same tone of badinage. 'The mediaeval gentleman,' he added, turning to me, 'who walked about with a sword stuck through his chest was easily the worst. Really, Dicky, you ought to get him exorcised.'

'Most people,' said I, 'prefer him to the Jacobean lady who wrings her hands.'

'Oh,' he answered, 'she was only on duty for about five minutes. Rotten lot of ghosts you keep here. Four of them and not a decent hollow groan between the lot.'

I think Muriel was a little disappointed at her Mystery Room having apparently failed to provide our guest with an uncanny experience. After breakfast she collared one of the grooms and drove over to Gaybury to do some shopping. Arthur, I knew, would have liked to go with her, but he had to put up with my society instead for the morning.

I subjected him to the usual infliction which a guest has to endure when paying his first visit to a country house, particularly when the property is still a new toy to his host. I showed him round. Together we inspected fields and farms, cattle and horses and pig-sties.

I noticed that he yawned several times and thought it rather unfriendly of him to be bored. As we were crossing a field of stubble I said to him suddenly:

'You look rather tired, old man. Is this boring you to death?'

'No, it's not that, but I am a bit tired,' he admitted.

'What's the matter? Didn't you sleep well?'

'Not very,' he replied, 'but then I never do for the first time in a strange room. I always have to be fagged out before I can drop off to sleep at an hotel, for instance.'

'No ghostly disturbances?' I asked, smiling.

'I was unusually restless,' he said, acknowledging my worn-out pleasantry with a faint smile, 'and I had very little sleep indeed. I'

He ended abruptly, and I saw his expression suddenly change. He was looking ahead into a grass field which we were approaching, and following the direction of his gaze I saw a cow with some strange malformation of one of its forelegs.

'Look at that brute of a cow!' he exclaimed in a voice which rang with disgust.

'I suppose it's nothing very serious, poor devil,' I said, 'or they'd have to have it destroyed.'

'I hate anything deformed or misshapen,' he said between his teeth, I could kill any monstrosity. I'd like to kill that infernal cow!'

I looked at him queerly. I thought I knew Arthur almost as well as I knew myself, and I was a little surprised, not so much at the words but at the tone in which they were uttered. I had previously heard him express repugnance for anything freakish or malformed, but it had always been repugnance mingled with pity. But his tone and expression now implied hatred, a passionate, bitter hatred. For a moment I saw Cruelty peeping out of his eyes. This was very strange, and—it wasn't Arthur!

A moment later, he laughed and said: 'I know you've always thought that there was a queer kink in me. We've all got our pet abominations.'

This was the first straw which afterwards showed me which way the wind had begun to blow. A strange depression settled on me for the rest of the morning. I had an uncomfortable suspicion that Arthur was not the fellow I thought he was, that there was a bad streak in him somewhere, of which for the first time he had just given me a glimpse.

During the next week, when Arthur and I were pretty constantly together, I saw, or thought I saw, a number of little changes in him, probably because I had set myself to look for them. He had not sought as much of Muriel's society as I had expected, and seemed to look more to me for companionship. He had been with us exactly a week when there came a sudden sequence of happenings which shook me more than a little.

I had just finished dressing for dinner, that is to say, except for my tie. I could always tie my own bows at a pinch, but I always preferred somebody else to do them for me, as my own efforts were never too successful. I never kept a valet, but one of the men had a spare-time job of brushing my clothes and putting them away. Arthur had lately been knotting my tie for me, so I went round to his room.

But this evening he had forgotten my needs and gone downstairs, so I walked along to Muriel's room and called to her to come out. She came out promptly, and I was shocked and surprised to see that she was crying. But in the midst of her tears she was smiling, and I heard her utter a little puzzled laugh.

'I don't know what's the matter with me, Dicky,' she said before I could utter a word, it all came on me just a moment ago. I felt so terribly sorry for something.'

'Sorry for what?' I exclaimed.

i don't know.' She laughed again and dabbed at her eyes. 'That's the absurd part of it. I feel that I've seen somebody in the most dreadful trouble, and—well, of course, I haven't!'

Now Muriel was never an emotional or imaginative sort of girl, and I thought I saw through a rather shallow artifice. I came to the conclusion that she had had some row with Arthur which neither of them had told me about. However, to humour her and not let her see what I suspected, I said: 'What an extraordinary girl you are, Muriel! Has anything of the sort ever happened to you before?'

'Yes,' she answered after a moment's hesitation, 'two or three times in the last few days, generally when I've been going to bed. I've had a most intense feeling of pity come over me. I don't mean depression, Dicky. I mean pity. For some reason or other I believe my nerves have all gone to pieces.'

'You with nerves, Muriel!' I exclaimed.

'Well, what else can it be? There seems to be something that seems to nudge up against me, something terror-stricken, that comes to me for protection, and looks to me for pity and love. That's how I feel. And if that isn't a case of nerves, I should like to know what is!'

'My dear old girl,' I said seriously, 'you'd better see a doctor tomorrow.'

But I am afraid I didn't feel as serious as my voice implied. I still thought that she was throwing dust in my eyes to prevent my seeing that she had had some misunderstanding with Arthur. But if that were the case, I couldn't help wondering why Arthur hadn't told me, or why he hadn't left us.

I went down to dinner pretty thoughtfully that night. I had noticed some subtle changes in Arthur, and I hated the feeling that there were many things of which I knew nothing going on around me below the surface.

We had been spending very quiet evenings. Generally Muriel played and sang to us for a little while and then went early to bed. Arthur and I generally played a hundred up, and were in our rooms before eleven. This evening was no exception as regards Muriel's departure.

I followed her up the stairs about two minutes later, for I wanted to show Arthur a letter I had just received from an old friend of ours, left in the pocket of a coat which I had discarded before dinner. I had reached the landing when I suddenly heard Muriel's voice from the passage leading to her room.

'Oh, you poor, poor darling,' it said. 'What is it then? What is the matter with you?'

I thought she was talking to some stray cat which had found its way into the house. She spoke in that crooning tone in which she addressed animals. But what she had told me before dinner was fresh in my mind, and I hastened to the comer of the passage.

There was no light burning in the passage, and the only illumination was a dull glow from the night skies diffused through the long row of windows. Muriel was standing about half-way down the passage, her head slightly bent as if she were in search of something. And I saw, or thought I saw, something crouching against her skirt, something broken and misshapen, but not inhuman; something in an attitude of terror and supplication.

It was gone even as my heart leaped at the sight. A moment later I could scarcely have said what I thought I saw. What it actually was I could not guess; a trick of the eyes perhaps, or part of Muriel's shadow which had fallen strangely in the dim light.

'Muriel!' I cried sharply.

She started, turned, and came towards me. There was distress visible in every step, in every movement of her slim body. When she had come up to me she touched my sleeves with her hands, as a child waking from a bad dream might touch something solid and comforting.

'Oh!' she gasped, and I felt her breath fan my face.

'What's the matter, Muriel?' I asked, and my voice sounded dry and troubled.

'It came over me again—that feeling. Something tortured by fear was fawning upon me for pity and protection. Can't you feel it too? No, I can see you can't. What does it mean, Dicky? Am I going mad?'

'You are going straight to bed,' I said, 'and tomorrow we will get a good doctor to run the rule over you. Something's happened to your nerves.'

'Yes, I know that,' she agreed drearily. 'But it's over now, for the time being. I'm quite all right again now.' She smiled tremulously, i know I'm worrying you, Dicky, and I'm so sorry. Perhaps I shall be better tomorrow.'

Now that I was convinced of the truth of what she had previously told me I was hard put to it to know what I had best do. To make a fuss, to suggest that she ought not to be alone, might only have the effect of frightening her into the belief that she was worse than she was. I did suggest that she should send for her maid, but she shook her head.

'I'm going straight to bed,' she said, it won't come over me again tonight. Goodnight, Dicky.'

She kissed me, took a step away from me, and then looked hurriedly back. 'Dicky! You won't say anything to Arthur about this, will you?'

'Of course not,' I said.

I went downstairs feeling pretty bad. That the bright and practical Muriel should show symptoms of a diseased imagination was something I had to dread. Here was no neurotic from whom one might expect an occasional mental relapse. I don't mind admitting now that the dreadful word Madness began to whisper itself to me, and would not be shaken from my mind. Arthur read the letter which I had brought to show him, and we chatted awhile over its contents.

'Going to play me a hundred up?' he asked at last.

I nodded, and we went into the billiard-room. Neither of us was a great performer, and tonight we were worse than usual. After a quarter of an hour we were still in the twenties, and Arthur at last, having missed an absurdly easy losing hazard, laid down his cue.

'Let's chuck this, shall we?' he said. 'We're both hopeless. Besides, I want to talk to you before I turn in.'

I went to the rack to put away my cue, and he came and stood, hands in pockets, close behind me, resting his back against the table.

'Dicky,' he said suddenly, 'I don't know how to put this to you. Do you know, when I came down here, I came with the intention of asking Muriel to marry me?'

i did suspect something of the sort,' I answered dryly.

'And I haven't done it. I wonder if you can guess why.'

During a bad moment I wondered if he knew of the change in Muriel.

'Old man,' he said in a shaken voice, i wonder if you've noticed anything peculiar about me?'

Well, I had; but apart from his little outburst out in the fields my impressions were all too vague to wear a label. So I said No.

'The fact is,' he said with a sort of dreary calmness, 'I have every reason to believe that I am going mad.'

So that was it. And there were two mad people in the house instead of one! I'm afraid my 'Nonsense, Arthur!' did not ring quite true.

i don't mean that I'm dangerous,' he continued quietly; 'at least, not to you or Muriel, or I should have put myself out of harm's way before this.'

Then his voice suddenly rose. 'But you show me anything ugly or deformed, and by God I could tear out its heart!'

As he spoke his fingers hooked involuntarily and his eyes dilated.

'Dicky,' he said, in a lower tone, 'have you ever known me to be cruel?'

'You're about the last man,' I said.

'Well, I'm not now. I could be hellishly cruel. I could be a devil to anything misshapen. I lie awake at night, imagining my fingers around the throat of a cringing hunchback. Yes, I don't wonder that you look at me like that. That isn't me, you know, Dicky.'

'It certainly isn't,' I agreed.

Back into my mind came the memory of the shadowy thing I thought I had seen crouching against Muriel's skirt in the passage.

'When did all this begin?' I asked.

'When I arrived here. I remember telling you I didn't sleep very well that first night. Well, lying awake, I got a sort of obsession. You know how I've always shrunk from the grotesque? I found myself actively hating something that was misshapen—not the hatred that one might have for an enemy, but a sort of frenzied abhorrence mixed up with—I don't know how to put it—a sort of personal grudge. And this hatred varied between all malformed beings and some particular personality which I imagined. I'm sorry to be so vague, and I'm afraid I've shocked you, Dicky. Believe me, I don't like myself a bit.'

I felt chilly and uncomfortable as I listened. I could not help remembering that this thing had come upon him in that room which Uncle Wilby had shut up. And back across the years came the vague memory of a story of his about a hunchback youth who had been done to death in this very house. Had he made up the story? Or was it true? And again, there was the strange shadow I had seen. All against my will my thoughts were leading me across the frontier of a strange territory.

'And have the same thoughts been tormenting you ever since?' I asked.

'Yes, but with a difference. My hatred has been directed almost entirely against this one particular personality. I can see it at times, but not with these eyes.' He pointed at his eyes with an excited gesture, it's a crookback idiot who's terrified of me, and yet he's always close by me at night, as if he can't get away. The terror of the thing and its slobbering inanity simply infuriate me. I've gone around my room, slashing with the poker, hoping to smash in its ugly skull, and always just missing the slobbering thing that blubbers and flinches and runs away from me. And all the while the saner side of me knows that it isn't there.' He uttered a short mirthless laugh. 'Well, what do you think of me, Dicky?'

'I think,' I said, 'that you ought to see a mental specialist at once.'

'Meaning that I oughtn't to stay on here? All right, I'll go tomorrow. Only it'll go with me, and I thought I had more chance of fighting it here, living with you and Muriel.'

What was that nebulous Something for which Muriel was moved to pity? Something that went from him to her for love and protection? Or was I too going mad?

'Wait a moment, old man,' I said. 'We'll suspend our judgement a bit before we decide that there's anything wrong with your head. You're pretty self-critical for a man with a mental disease. Most men afflicted in that way don't know it. Do you think it's the room which has caused all this?'

'The room?' he repeated. 'What can the room have to do with it?'

'It was shut up, and very likely with a purpose. Uncle Wilby may have slept there for all I know, and come under the same sort of influence. I remember his telling us a story once about a hunchback youth who was murdered in this very house.'

'Oh, ghosts again!' he exclaimed impatiently. 'My dear Dicky, I simply don't believe in that sort of thing. And I don't see anything—at least not in the accepted sense of the term.'

'It's strange I should have heard the story of a hunchback being killed in this house.'

'Not a bit! I'd have killed him myself!' His eyes dilated again, and he clenched his hands until his biceps quivered with the strain, if only this thing which obsesses me were living, tangible, Dicky, I'd tear it to pieces!'

I am quite incapable of reproducing his tone or giving the least impression of it. It literally chilled my blood.

'Arthur,' I said, I'm coming with you to your room. I want to see if I too am affected in any way.'

In Arthur's room I sat in an armchair by the fireplace, and he sat on the edge of the bed.

'I don't feel that way now,' he said quite calmly; 'or, if you prefer it, it isn't here. You'll feel nothing, Dicky, unless I infect you with my madness. You'd better go before I get worked up. I warn you I shan't be a pretty sight.'

'At all events I'll wait,' I said.

One can form theories very quickly, and I had already blundered a little way on the right track. I did not expect to be affected in the same way as Arthur. I never had, to begin with, his artistic sense of repulsion for what was freakish. Neither had I Muriel's keen sense of pity for those so afflicted. These different senses in them both had, it seemed to me, been intensified and distorted. It was as if both of them shared, in a sense, the same thought.

Here was Arthur hating and loathing and longing to do violence to something imaginary. There was Muriel, pitying at the same time something imaginary which came to her as if for love and protection.

We sat on smoking in silence for a long while, during which my thoughts raced ahead of me, and had to be called back from all sorts of mental labyrinths. And suddenly I began to notice that Arthur was getting uneasy.

Presently he slipped down from the edge of the bed.

'Are you?' I began.

I couldn't find the words I wanted to complete the question, but I knew he understood. He took no notice of me, however. He was staring into a comer of the room by the floor, and I saw his eyes kindle and his upper lip lift with the lust of hatred. Then from his mouth came hissing a string of lewd epithets. The change in the man, from one of the best fellows in the world to a devil incarnate, was as sudden as it was startling and beastly.

I have seen a man in delirium tremens, but his behaviour was nothing compared with that of Arthur's. Still glaring malevolently at the comer, in which I could see nothing, he sidled to the grate and picked up the poker. Then, suddenly springing, he slashed wildly at the empty air.

'I'll have you yet!' he breathed in a dreadful whisper. 'You foul, elusive beast! I'll smash . . . and smash . . . and smash . . .'

He was slashing this way and that as he spoke, leaping about the room, dodging and wheeling. The poker hummed in the air as he struck and struck. Under one of these blows the brass rail at the foot of the bed smashed like a glass tube. I sat like a man transfixed, unable to move or speak, as I watched that ghastly pantomime.

Suddenly he made a dash for the door as if in pursuit of something. He wrenched it open with one jerk of the hand and arm and was out and across the landing. Then I found a use for my limbs and followed him.

He was running towards the passage leading to Muriel's room, cursing and flourishing the poker as he ran. And as I turned the comer behind him, I saw Muriel standing fully dressed outside her door.

What else I saw I saw but very dimly; but I swear I saw it. Crouching against her, its brow touching her instep, was the grotesque figure of a hunchback dwarf, in the same attitude in which I had seen it before. And on the instant Muriel's voice rang out.

'Don't, Arthur! Don't! Oh, don't hurt him for my sake, Arthur!'

He had his back to me, but I was somehow as well aware of the sudden change wrought in him as if I had seen his face. He seemed to trip and stumble into a walk. He ceased to brandish the poker, letting it swing gently for a moment, and then dropping it almost noiselessly upon the carpet.

'Muriel!' he said, in a queer, strangled sort of voice.

It seemed that to those two, who had never previously uttered a word of love, had suddenly been given a perfect understanding. When he reached her he took her quite naturally into his arms, and the Shape at her feet melted away like mist from a glass.

The house was no place for either of them. We all three went away on the morrow to Bournemouth, and while we were there we reasoned the thing out amongst us as best we could. Arthur and Muriel were both quite normal as soon as they had left the house. Muriel had been feeling too upset to go to bed that night, and had had a sudden impulse to rush out of her room and protect the Thing that had been seeking her pity and protection when she met us both in the passage.

Now we all three decided that Uncle Wilby's story about the hunchback was at least founded on fact. At some time during the history of the house some afflicted youth had been sent here to be murdered. Probably the poor wretch more than suspected his fate, and his terror whetted the hatred of the fiend who subsequently murdered him.

We agreed that the murder probably took place in the room in which Arthur had slept, and that certain forces had lain dormant there ever since—fiendish hatred and loathing on the one hand and gibbering terror on the other.

People of certain temperaments who used the room were liable to be affected. There was Arthur, with his natural repulsion for what Nature had mis-made, an easy victim to the force that overwhelmed him. His hatred re-created an object in the spirit of the poor murdered youth, who fled for pity and succour to the kindest and sweetest spirit in the house. Perhaps in those last terrible days of his life there had been a woman in the house who pitied him and yet could not save him.

It is almost useless to theorise over these things. We shall never know in this world.

When we returned I had the walls of that bedroom taken down, and in one of them we found the bones of a boy or an undersized man. They were not the bones of a normally shaped person.

Arthur and Muriel married, as you know, and you don't need me to tell you that Arthur is one of the best fellows in the world, without a spark of cruelty in his composition.

I don't think it would hurt anybody to sleep in that room now. We don't keep it shut up, but we don't put people in there. I don't believe in taking risks.

And now I think I've propounded a riddle which it would puzzle any materialist to answer.

The Imperturbable Tucker

It could only have happened in a large town parish, whose ill-defined boundaries were known only to the vicar and the parish clerk, if even to them. And it happened on Christmas Eve, which means that the weather was muggy and wet, and that everybody with any desire or pretensions to sing carols—and many who had neither—were out and after their neighbours' legal tender.

The official carol singers, comprising certain male voices from the church choir, led by Mr Thomas Tucker, were, of course, doing better business than their rivals.

The reasons for this were many and good. The noises they produced were less painful to sensitive ears. They had locus standi. And where Mr Tucker observed no symptoms of generosity he was able to plead that all the monies were to be handed direct to a most deserving cause.

Apart from the facts that he had a baritone voice of sorts, and could reach the compass of a sailor having teeth out without gas, there seemed no very good reason why Thomas Tucker should be a member of the church choir.

Many people questioned why he was, although the answer was quite simple. It was simply because he was a creature of habit and had been made to join the choir as a small boy. His mother had conveyed him to all the practices by the left ear—which even now protruded a little more than the right—until the habit was so engrafted on him that he could be trusted to go alone.

For similar reasons he was now a butcher. He had been apprenticed to the trade in days when his fancy had lightly turned to the High Seas and to deeds of doubtful ethics under a flag which he was wont to call the Jolly Ole Roger. He had become a full-blown butcher simply because everybody else connected with that particular shop had died, and because he had heard that the only pirates left were certain Asiatic gentlemen who lived principally on rats, birds' nests, and unwanted dogs.

He was not only a person with whom habit soon became unalterable nature, but one to whom nothing came amiss. He was phlegmatic as a waxwork figure, and people said that it was impossible to shock, surprise, or scare him. How true this may be the reader must presently judge for himself. Tucker and his band of singers had been out some two hours ere they came to a curious old house, once of some pretensions, hiding away from its new and perky neighbours behind a red wall enclosing a bedraggled garden. Two or three members of the choir halted before the rusty gate and debated as to whether the house came within the parish boundary.

'Doesn't matter,' said Tucker. 'People who live in it won't know either.'

And he pushed open the creaking gate and led the procession up the path. They formed a semicircle in front of the hall door of the dingy old house that showed not a light anywhere.

'I believe it's empty,' said the leading tenor.

'Soon see,' said Tucker. '"Good King Wenceslas".'

They got as far as the good king's lavish order for pine logs, when they suddenly stopped. Tucker finishing the verse alone. No lights had appeared, and all except Tucker were convinced that they were wasting their breath on an empty house.

Hoarsely they pointed out this probability once more to Tucker, who had otherwise, from force of habit, gone through with the carol to the bitter end and possibly begun another.

'Soon see,' said Tucker. 'Wait a sec.'

He strode to the steps and walked up to the door. There was a great black handle which slipped back under pressure, and Tucker pushed the door open before him.

'Don't be a fool!' hissed a voice. 'You can't walk in.'

'I have,' said Tucker, and he closed the door behind him.

At first it seemed to him that the house really was empty. There were no lights in the front rooms, as he had already seen from without, and the place smelt of dust and decay. But nothing less than a complete inspection of the premises would satisfy him; and largesse would certainly be demanded of any human being.

He was on his way to the servants' quarters when he noticed that a door on his left was thinly framed by a bluish light stealing through its chinks. Tucker pushed open the door without knocking and entered the room beyond. The room was small and almost devoid of furniture. It was lit by a candle which burned strangely, and gave the wan bluish light which had attracted him.

In a far corner a villainous-looking old man was on his knees before a great chest. The old man was clad in rags, and the wicked leering face above his dirty white beard would have inspired a mediaeval designer of gargoyles. But in spite of his rags the chest was full of gold pieces which ran like sand through his long, crooked fingers, and chinked wickedly as they dropped. The scene was weird enough, and sufficiently awe-inspiring to appal the stoutest heart.

'Evenin',' said Tucker.

The old man's wicked eyes blazed at him.

'Stranger,' he said in deep, hollow tones, 'what do you here?'

'Collecting,' said Tucker. 'Ain't you heard the carol-singers?'

'No!'

'Ah, you ought to have been round in the front. Will you go round or shall I bring 'em in here?'

'Do you know whom you address?' cried the old man in an awful voice.

'I am Devloe, the miser.'

'Pleased to meet you,' said Tucker. 'Subscriptions, however small, are invited. You don't seem to have anything less than Jimmy O'Goblins in that box. So much the better.'

'You will get nought from me,' cried the old man angrily,

'I bet I do. Buck up. Then we'll sing to you. Will you have "Noel" or "Hark the Herald"?'

'The only music I delight in is the tinkling of these little coins which are my heart's blood to me.'

'Quite nice,' Tucker agreed, 'I wish I had a few of 'em. Come on. It's Christmas time, and this is a good cause.'

'Never,' cried the old man, 'have I ever given anything away.'

'Time you did, then,' said Tucker.

'This is tainted gold.'

'Can't help that,' said Tucker. 'We've got two company promoters in our congregation, and there'd be a row if the verger didn't pass 'em the plate.'

'Every penny of this was wrung from the poor'

'And I bet it wanted some wringing,' said Tucker. 'You ought to see the money I've got out on my books.'

'Except what was stolen by violence.'

'Ah, that's easier,' said Tucker.

'I have committed bigamy, theft, arson, forgery.'

'Really,' said Tucker, faintly interested.

'And two murders!' thundered the old man.

'You have been a bit of a nib, haven't you?' said Tucker agreeably. 'But think what a comfort it will be to you to know that you've contributed'

A look of hopelessness dawned in the old man's wicked eyes.

'Will nothing frighten you away from here?' he demanded.

'Not that I know of.'

'And you will not go?'

'Not until you've subscribed'

The old man interrupted him with a loud groan.

'Take a coin, then,' he said resignedly. 'Stay, I will find you the smallest. Anything to get rid'

'Hold hard,' said Tucker. 'You needn't be mean about it. Remember it's for an excellent cause.'

'What cause?'

'The Church Warming Fund,' said Tucker.

A terribly cry emanated from the top of the old man's beard. He dropped the lid of the chest and held it down as firmly as he could with his thin hands.

'Look here!' he exclaimed. 'There are limits, you know. I told you the kind of life I led. Well, I died years ago, and if you think I'm going to subscribe to any kind of warming fund'

Words suddenly failed him, and so, seemingly, did everything else. The light and the apparition—for an apparition Tucker now knew it to be—vanished in a flash.

'There now!' Tucker murmured.

He lingered to strike a match and see if the treasure chest had also vanished.

Finding that it had, he murmured, 'There's a pity!' and went out to rejoin his fellow carol-singers.

'Any luck?' someone shouted, as he reappeared.

Tucker shook his head. 'Found an old man, but I couldn't get nothing out of him.'

'Why didn't you tell 'im to go to blazes?' somebody demanded.

'Wasn't necessary,' said Tucker. 'Come on. Next house.'

The Wind in the Attic

If you do that,' said Grant, 'your queen is dead.'

Old Treves, white-haired, delicate-handed, thin almost to gauntness, unclosed his long pallid fingers from the pawn.

'Never mind,' he said. 'I have made my move.'

'It will spoil the game,' said Grant, hesitating.

He looked up to see that Treves had not heard. The old man sat back in his chair, his gaze indeed on the board, but his attention elsewhere.

'Very well,' said Grant after a moment, 'if you insist on playing strictly according to the rules.'

'Strictly according to the rules,' murmured the old man. 'Strictly according'

'Check.'

'Eh?' Treves leaned forward once more and peered about among his scattered defences. 'Check, eh?'

'It is mate in two moves now. You should have taken back that pawn when I gave you the chance. You can only go here. Then I bring my rook up here. Then you go there, and I take that pawn with my queen and say checkmate.'

The older man followed this line of reasoning and inclined his head.

Then, one by one, he began to remove the pieces.

'You are too good for me,' he said, it is very rarely that I have beaten you.'

'We are very well matched when you are in the mood.'

Treves did not answer. He had lapsed once more into preoccupation. His eyes were slightly upturned. His whole attitude suggested that he was listening for some sound.

'You do not wish to play any more?' said Grant.

'Pardon?'

'You do not wish to play again?'

The old man smiled gently. 'If you do not mind. Chess is such a tax on the brain. As I grow older. . . .Ah, the wind is freshening.'

The windows rattled. Outside the chestnut trees rustled as if under a fall of rain. In a moment the night had become full of mournful voices.

Grant turned in his chair and stretched out his hands to the fire, although they were not cold. He was an iron-grey, middle-aged man, practical in most things as became a bank manager. What was artistic in his nature had turned towards music and made a church organist of him.

'You don't like to hear the wind?' asked old Treves.

'I am getting to an age when there is no pleasure in melancholy. And I don't require extraneous aids to it.'

Another gust of breeze shook the windows. And now there were sounds on the floor above, as if the wind were a live thing which had entered the house and was wandering, lost and frightened, among strange rooms. One succession of sounds was like a quick pattering of little feet.

Grant looked across at Treves and saw him listening intently, his eyes upturned.

'And I think,' he continued, 'that I like hearing the wind in this house less than I like hearing it anywhere. What room is above this?'

'An attic,' murmured Treves. 'An attic. An old lumber room.'

'The wind makes queer noises there. Last time I came I thought I heard a child crying.'

Treves stared across at him almost angrily.

'Not crying!' he exclaimed in a hurt voice. 'Oh, not crying!' it sounded like that,' Grant said.

In the attic above the wind was still busy. The flapping blind sounded like the clapping of little hands. Another sound, made perhaps by the wind in the chimney, caused Grant to smile and nod at the older man.

'Did you hear that?' he asked. 'That was like children laughing.'

'Ah, laughing! Yes, yes. That's what I like to hear. And when they cry, you know, Grant, it doesn't always mean that they're in pain, or want something they can't have.'

A vague feeling of discomfort stole over Grant.

'There aren't any children in the house,' he said.

He meant it as an assertion, but he heard a questioning ring in his own voice.

'Not to you,' said the old man.

Grant rose. The material side of him was up in arms, and he was a little annoyed at himself for feeling otherwise than completely comfortable.

'You ought to have something done to that attic,' he said. 'A decorator would put the place right so that you didn't hear those queer sounds. They are nothing, of course, but when one is living alone, as you are'—he tailed off lamely—'it must be bad for one's nerves,' he added.

The old man laughed softly.

I want them to be there,' he said. 'They know that. Always on windy nights … ah, listen!'

'He's mad,' thought Grant. 'Old and mad. Everybody knows it. It's nothing but . . . damn the wind.'

But he lingered, standing by the chimney comer, watching Treves, whose face wore a smile that was almost beautiful.

'Who are they?' he asked, a little ashamed of himself for putting the question.

Old Treves seemed not to hear. He was listening elsewhere, it's the wind!' said Grant almost irritably.

'Ah, they want you to think that. They know that I know.'

'Do you mean to tell me,' the organist stuttered, 'that there are real children up in that attic?'

'Real children,' murmured the old man. 'Very real children. You don't believe? What is that to me? I believe. I know.'

Grant drew a deep breath. The strongest sceptic concerning things unearthly may be permitted to feel uncomfortable when alone in a house with an old madman on a windy night.

'Have you ever seen them?' he asked, as if trying to probe the depth of the other's madness.

'No. Sometimes they creep downstairs from the attic and cluster about the door, and whisper outside, and peep at me through the chinks. But when I open the door they are gone. They can run very quickly—my little children.'

'Funny you only hear them on windy nights,' said Grant.

'Ah, you've forgotten what it is to be shy. When your body was small you were shy, you know. But supposing you never had a body? You'd only dare to play with your brothers and sisters, when fools might mistake your laughter for the wind in the chimney, and the clapping of your hands for the beating of a loose blind.'

As he ceased speaking there was a riot of minute sounds overhead, so like the pattering of children's feet and the low gurgling of children's laughter that Grant felt a stirring in the roots of his hair.

'It's all rubbish!' he cried angrily. 'Your children! You never had any! Oh, get something done to that attic! It's bad for you! It's unhealthy!'

The old man laughed gently and rubbed his thin hands.

'You're a Christian, my friend,' he said. 'You play the organ in church. I have seen you kneeling in prayer. Do you then deny you have a soul?'

'No.'

'And when did you first have it?'

'How should I know? These things are mysteries.'

'And suppose, my friend, your body had never been born, what of your soul, then?'

The organist shifted his feet uncomfortably. He had heard before of men who were logical in their madness. He fell back upon his old ground, and held it defiantly.

'It's the wind upstairs,' he said.

The old man disregarded the words.

'I never married,' he said. 'She died two months before the day. Our children who were never born . . . you hear them now . . .'

His voice trailed into silence, and Grant, about to rail at him for voicing something which was opposed to human reason, suddenly checked himself. He realised that this forlorn old man had stumbled upon a creed which had comfort in it. A few crumbs had fallen to him from the world's loaded tables.

The wind in the attic had given him food for dreams.

Who was he. Grant asked himself, that he should snatch comfort from one who needed it so sorely? A kindly and mysterious Providence had given the old man those dreams which the opium-smoker seeks. He answered sympathetically:

'I am sorry. I did not know. Some day I hope you will see them.'

The old man shook his head.

'Not until the end,' he said, i am sure of that now. Right at the end. God willing . . .'

As an unimaginative man, it was seldom that Grant had reason to blame his nerves. But a little later, when he opened the door to go out, and a broad flash of light fell athwart the darkened landing, he could have sworn he heard a sudden scurry of little feet up the stairs leading to the attic. He raised his eyes with difficulty, for his heart had leapt, and the breath in his nostrils was chilled by a sudden shock. He looked and saw nothing.

It was about a fortnight later that Mr Widgeon, the vicar, buttonholed Grant in the High Street. It was a Monday morning, and the vicar had been around paying his weekly bills. A miniature parcel dangled from a string fastened to his little finger. He was a young vicar, and so comparatively fresh from Oxford that he was inclined to be frivolous in his conversation.

'Ha, Grant,' he said, 'a little bird has been telling me something.'

'Meaning a parrot?' Grant enquired.

'Ha, ha! Good! Very good! No, no, Grant, one of my spies, I mean. We have spies in the parish, you know. I employ a secret service.'

'And you've had a report about me?' Grant asked.

'Yes, a report about you. But nothing very dreadful. I hear that the last month or two you've been admitted into the house of our hermit. Succeeded where I and Canon Robson, who was here before me, have both failed. He wouldn't let either of us into the house.'

'You're speaking of old Mr Treves?' said Grant.

'Who else? We haven't many hermits in this part of the world. We are a gregarious people.'

'I've been there about twice a week for the last month,' said Grant, 'playing chess with him.'

'So the little bird told me,' giggled the vicar. 'How did you manage it? I called on him in the usual way when I was installed here. I'd seen him regularly at church, and felt it my duty to go and look him up. He was quite civil, but he wouldn't let me into the house. Canon Robson had the same experience. How did you contrive it?'

Grant smiled to himself. He knew that he was being pumped. Old Treves was a local celebrity, about whom a hundred stories, mostly untrue, were current. Gossip was the breath of life to the giggling, good-natured, rather frivolous Mr Widgeon.

'It didn't come about by my seeking,' said Grant. 'I was playing the organ in the church one Sunday afternoon when I thought I was alone. I didn't hear him come in, but he was there when I went out, and he stopped and spoke to me. He said something kind about my playing, and then asked me if I played chess. When I told him I did, he surprised me by asking me round.'

They had fallen into step together, and were making their way by slow paces down the street.

'Does he play well?' the vicar inquired.

'Yes—when all his attention is on the game. He'd been playing alone for years, working out chess problems set in old newspapers. Sometimes, though, he seems to be thinking of other things.'

'Ah, yes.' The vicar nodded comprehendingly. 'I wonder what the house is like inside?'

'Rather stuffy furniture—mid-Victorian stuff. A little untidy, as you would expect. On the whole, though, he seems to manage very well by himself. It's rather a large house. These square-fronted, stone Georgian houses are larger inside than one would imagine.'

The vicar nodded again. His expression was one of slight disappointment. It was as if he had not heard all that he wished to hear. He felt that Grant, in seeming to answer his questions frankly and fully, was somehow fencing with him.

'Isn't there some romance about him?' hazarded Mr Widgeon.

'Something dating back a long time? A love story, or something, that broke him up? I've heard rumours about it.'

'I daresay,' said Grant blandly. He did not feel inclined to betray what he felt to be a confidence.

The vicar uttered a little baffled laugh.

'Ah, Grant,' he said, i see you can tell the difference between gold and silver where speech and silence are concerned. Well, well, one shouldn't be too curious, I suppose. I have always been sorry for the poor old man. He's aged very rapidly in the last year or two. Breaking up, I fear.'

'I shouldn't wonder. He must be very old.'

'Of course,' said Mr Widgeon, sinking his voice confidentially, 'he's always been very—er—eccentric is the kindest term to use. But don't you think he—eh?' He coughed, and indicated a more advanced mental trouble by an upward glance and a slight and delicate gesture.

'I don't know that I should say that,' replied the organist.

'Well, I don't want to interfere. If the old man is harmless, there is no reason why he should be put away. But I saw something very odd the day before yesterday. I was in Baldwin's, the toyshop, buying a doll for my young niece. To my astonishment old Treves was in there, too, and he'—here the vicar giggled slightly—'he was buying a big box of soldiers.'

Grant started slightly, but said nothing.

'I—er—made some inquiries there after he was gone,' continued the vicar, 'and found that he was in the habit of buying toys there—soldiers and trains and dolls. What does he do with them?'

'I suppose,' said Grant loyally, 'he gives them away to poor children.'

'Either that, or he plays with them himself. Poor old man, one oughtn't to laugh!'

'He may have some young relatives to whom he sends them.'

'I have never heard of any. And I don't believe he gives them to the poor. The whole neighbourhood would know about it if he did. Well, well, it's very sad. But so long as he's quite harmless ... ah, I see you are in a hurry. I mustn't detain you any longer, Mr Grant. See you at Evensong? Goodbye, goodbye!'

It was apparent to all who saw him abroad that old Treves was failing rapidly. And when the hand of winter fell heavily upon the land, its icy fingers took hard hold at the frail figure which the little township knew so well by sight. He was not seen for two days, and then Grant, calling and failing to attract attention by knocking and ringing, took the liberty of breaking in. He found the old man lying, fully dressed, on his bed, and scarcely breathing. Within an hour a doctor and the district nurse had invaded the premises.

The doctor shook his head at Grant in answer to the organist's inquiry.

'He's worn out. When the human engine is worn out there is only one thing that can happen. A man can't get a new heart.'

'How long?' asked Grant.

The doctor shrugged his shoulders.

'Perhaps a couple of days. Perhaps not so long.'

But the old man lasted three, and during that period Grant called three or four times a day, and received the same answers to his inquiries.

At the end of the third day, when the street lamps were alight and an icy wind was blowing over the iron-bound land, the nurse, who came quietly to the door in answer to his knock, beckoned him inside.

'He is conscious,' she whispered, 'and asked to see you if you called. Will you come up?'

A great fire was burning in the sick-room, and the atmosphere of it was oven-like to Grant after the cold outside. Treves's face lay pressed into a pillow, the only part of him visible in the huddle of bedclothes. It looked thinner and frailer than ever, and he lay quite motionless, but the light of consciousness was in his eyes. As Grant stood regarding him a little embarrassed, the lips moved.

'Bend closer over him,' said the nurse.

Grant bent, and heard a scarcely audible whisper.

'Under my pillow.....the key.'

The organist groped under the pillow, and his hand encountered the cold iron of a large key. He knew that it was the key of the attic. Once more he bent his ear close to the lips of the dying man.

'I am ready now....waiting....go and tell them.'

Grant nodded comprehendingly, rose, and turned towards the door. The raised brows of the nurse asked a question of him.

'It's all right,' he murmured. 'I understand.'

The wind was at play in the attic as he mounted the stairs. He could hear the sounds that had grown familiar to him on windy nights, and had to fight hard against a sensation of eeriness which clogged his steps.

'It's all rubbish,' he muttered through his teeth. 'An old man's fancy . . .poor old chap.'

He fitted the key into the lock and turned it. And, as he entered, the wind lulled and a great quiet was in the room. The sudden silence shocked him as if a hand had touched him. He groped in his pocket for matches, found them, and struck one with trembling fingers. The pale flame climbing the stick, lit up the room.

It was full of old lumber, broken furniture, the accumulation of years, but as the match died out, he saw that the floor was littered with toys, and struck another. The silence was so complete that the spurt of the match startled him.

Rival armies of lead soldiers faced each other on the floor, which was thick with the dust of thirty years. On the left a train was drawn into a toy station close by a great dolls' house.So, after all, the old man had been playing with his toys.

But had he? Had he? For more than three days he had not moved, and the train had left double tracks—fresh tracks—in the dust of the floor where it had been drawn across. The lead soldiers, too, had made fresh tracks, where one army had advanced and another fallen back. But who had moved them? Who, in God's name, had moved them?

The flame of the match climbed up and burnt one of Grant's fingers. He dropped it with a little cry, and lit another to stare once more upon the miracle. His mind was befogged, and vaguely he was fighting against the evidence of his sight.

'I won't believe!' he said fiercely aloud, it's all monstrous! I won't believe!'

But, believing or not, he obeyed the charge of the dying man.

'Children,' he said, and his voice was all low and soft and strained, 'children, your father wants you. He says he's ready now—ready and waiting. Go and fetch him.'

Having spoken, he spun about on his heels and faced the door, his heart galloping with sudden panic. It seemed to him that the stillness of the room was broken by more than the sound of his own movements—incoherent sounds, subtly suggestive of small people crowding to the door and pushing past him. Ahead of him he could hear a stealthy jostling on the stairs. Keeping a tight hold on himself, he refrained from running, but walked slowly down and back into the sick-room.

As he entered he could not rid himself of the feeling that others had entered just before him, and to this day he is still in doubt.

The nurse looked up as he entered. Then she laid the tips of two fingers upon her lips.

The Garden of Fancy

I cannot clearly recall how the conversation began; I only remember that we suddenly found ourselves immersed in a topic which has a great fascination for all who own to a strain of mysticism. We spoke of people who dreamed vividly of houses, villages, and even towns which they had never been to, and dreamed so vividly that they were familiar with the smallest details of their visionary haunts.

It was a Sunday afternoon, and the club lounge was deserted except for the four of us who were weekend visitors to London. We were something more than mere club acquaintances, and it was a happy chance which had thus drawn us together to dispel one another's boredom.

'I think I know what you fellows mean,' said Pewsey, the artist, absently filling a pipe. 'Chap comes to a strange place, stares, and exclaims: "Why, I've been here before!" And yet he knows he hasn't. That's not at all uncommon'

'No, I don't mean that at all,' Ford interrupted, in fact, I mean just the opposite. Going to a strange place for the first time and recognising it may be put down to a hundred different causes. Inherited memory—that's a bit far-fetched, of course—but there's self-hypnotism, and the possibility of having seen and forgotten pictures of the place, or having heard it minutely described. In those cases a man does not remember the place. He only thinks he recognises it when he sees it. We're speaking of people who dream in detail of places they have never been to'

'And afterwards find the places of their dreams?' Pewsey asked.

'Not necessarily. Indeed, I never heard of an instance. I believe these dream-places are always non-existent in fact.'

'Don't be so sure,' remarked Harlow, the novelist, I should have believed that these dream-places were non-existent if I hadn't had some personal experience.'

We all looked at him to see if he were smiling, as indeed he was, but it was not the smile he wore when he indulged in the gentle pastime of pulling legs.

'You mean,' asked Pewsey, 'that you dreamed of a place you had never seen nor heard of, and afterwards you actually saw it?'

'No, I don't mean that.'

'Then how can you say you've had personal experience?'

Harlow laughed good-naturedly.

'It sounds paradoxical, I know,' he remarked; 'but it is nevertheless true. I've often thought of making a short story of it, but I can't write short stories. I can only work satisfactorily on a large canvas. Besides, there are some important links missing which I don't suppose will ever be found. As it stands, the tale is only a jumble of queerness, unexplained, and, I truly believe, inexplicable. It seems wholly improbable; and, besides, people like their fiction neatly rounded off, without any loose ends—worked out and proved, like a sum in arithmetic.'

'Never mind,' drawled Ford, with a faint air of superiority, 'we aren't the public. Let's hear the story and judge for ourselves.'

'All right,' said Harlow good-naturedly; 'but I warn you, you won't believe me or be able to make head or tail of it. But it's solid fact; indeed, it was through this queer business that I first met my wife.'

We all laughed.

'Well, that's conventional enough for any work of fiction,' I remarked, 'I've read a hundred stories which began like that.'

'Yes,' said Harlow; 'but I'll wager they didn't end like this one. Well, if you want to hear, I suppose there's no harm in telling you.'

Although (said Harlow) I needn't inflict on you the whole story of my life, I am afraid it will be necessary to bore you with a few bits of autobiography. I was the only son of my parents, and my father was a retired Army man, and terribly poor. My people settled down in a pokey little six-roomed villa at Hewstone, in Berkshire, so that, when I grew old enough, they might contrive to send me to Hurlborough, which was my father's old school.

You know Hurlborough, of course. Some of the wealthiest families in the country had their sons there, but I should think, if the truth were known, there was a large proportion of boys whose parents had scraped and saved and made similar sacrifices to those made by my own father and mother. There always was and always will be a great deal of snobbery below the surface of a public school. The richer boys set a certain standard which the rest of us had to follow as best we could. Hardly any fellow exhibited the bad form to boast about his father's money, but, on the other hand, their poorer brethren lived in terror lest the poverty of their homes should be discovered. One never openly bragged, but one bragged by inference. One casually mentioned certain good times enjoyed during the holidays, which left it to be inferred that one's people had spent a lot of money. We saw through one another, but we respected one another's poses, always remembering our own.

Roughly, the school was divided into those who could say they had hunted or shot or been to Switzerland during the Christmas holidays, and those who could not. One was terrified lest one's father should arrive on Speech Day wearing the wrong kind of hat. I dare say things have altered now. I am speaking of long before the War. Nowadays it is rather chic to be poor. It wasn't then. A funny, snobbish, clannish lot of little beasts we were; in fact, we were just ordinary boys of an awkward age.

I made plenty of friends. Automatically we sorted ourselves into sets. And perhaps the boy I liked most, for no particular reason, was a youngster of my own age who bore the commonplace name of Thompson. He was in my House, played in the same games, began in the same division of the same Form as myself, and, while I remained, we moved up the school together. It was as well that we were friends, because circumstance had seemed to ordain that we were to be inseparable.

He was a small fat boy with one of those cheeky, good-natured faces which nobody can help taking to on sight. He had a natural gift for ragging which amounted almost to genius, and he was perpetually in hot water. A queer phenomenon he has always seemed to me—a natural clown with depths, intelligence, sympathy, and decent instincts. In any event I should always have remembered him as the coolest and most colossal liar I have ever met.

Don't misunderstand me. He was not an offensive liar. He never slandered, and he never lied with the least hope of being believed. I suppose really the offensive thing about a lie is the motive behind it. Thompson's motive was plainly to amuse. It was as if he had entered into a tacit bargain with the rest of us: it amused him to spin his yarns, and it amused us to listen. The only trouble was that if by any chance any of his milder reminiscences had some vague foundation on fact it was impossible to tell.

We knew that Thompson's father was a parson, and his status in the Church was a little vague, since Thompson sometimes described his reverend sire as a rector, sometimes as a dean, and sometimes as a suffragan bishop. As a matter of fact, the Reverend Mr Thompson was senior curate of a large church in a suburb of London, and poor as any of the mice which may have inhabited it. Thompson had very little to say about his father but plenty to say about his uncle, who was, by inference, a county magnate with almost incredible wealth.

'Oh,' Thompson would say, when asked where he was going to spend the next holidays, 'part of the time, I suppose, I shall be down at my uncle's place. It really is a ripping show. You ought to see it!' And his eyes would light up.

There was nothing Thompson enjoyed more than telling us about his uncle's place. He had quite a gift for describing things, and he described his uncle's place so often and so minutely that most of us knew it as if we had actually paid a visit there.

The house apparently stood with its left shoulder to the main entrance and quite close the road. There were huge wrought-iron gates which opened in the middle. Over them hung a shield of arms and a lamp. There was 'a funny kind of bird' on the shield. 'You ought to know what kind of bird it is,' I once said to Thompson, it must be your crest too, you know.'

Thompson shook his head. He could get out of most tight comers.

'Uncle on my mother's side, y'know. Named Villiers.'

To continue, the house was built of stone, but so smothered with creepers that you could hardly see it. It had five gables. If you went up the short drive you could, instead of going straight on up to the house, turn to the left and go down a walk with box trees on one side wonderfully cut. The first represented a peacock, the second a hippogriff, the third an acorn, and the fourth a giant mushroom. Going on further you came to a tennis court raised on a bank some five feet above the ordinary garden level. Those box trees took hold on my imagination, which is probably why I remembered his description of the garden in such minute detail.

Curiously enough, Thompson never described the inside of the house.

'Oh,' he would say, vaguely, 'it's all right inside!' When asked to say where this desirable property was situated, he would reply: 'Place called Little Lynn down in Hampshire. You wouldn't know it.'

I looked in vain for Little Lynn on the map, but I did find it in a novel which Thompson had been reading. This, you will say, exploded the myth so far as I was concerned. In a sense it did. But Thompson described the place so often, and never varied in his details, that I for one suspected a vague foundation on fact. My theory was that Thompson had actually seen such a house and gardens from the outside, and they had taken such a hold on his fancy that he had generously presented them, in imagination, to one of his uncles.

All this, it may be urged, is very trivial, and but for the sequel I should be wasting my breath and your attention. I want you to understand that Thompson told me about this old house and garden so often and in such minute detail that I never forgot it and could almost hypnotise myself into believing that I had seen them.

I left school before Thompson. My father's death when I was sixteen and a half necessitated my immediate removal. The state of the family exchequer made it necessary for me to begin to pull my weight. I had won an English prize, and I could write schoolboy essays, so I was naturally considered a heaven-born journalist. Within a month influence had obtained for me a berth on the Hewstone Weekly Argus. There I learned my trade, in a sort of way, and at twenty-one I got my chance in London on the Daily Leader.

I never really cared for journalism; I had always intended to be a novelist. Journalism provided me with bread-and-butter while I was learning the other craft. I had very little fun and very little recreation. All that time I hardly saw an Old Hurlburian, and hadn't the least idea what had become of old Thompson.

By the time I was twenty-five I had launched two novels on an unsuspecting world. I lost on both these because I had had to pay for the typing; and my publisher complained that he was ruined. Then, while I was still on the Leader I wrote White Sunday, and woke one morning to find myself in clover.

I don't know what made White Sunday go as it did. I've written better and worse since, but everything I've done that can be called a success, I owe to the success of that one book. It has always mystified me, and it almost frightened me at the time. From a month after the date of publication it started selling in thousands.

Well, there was I, a newspaper man earning six pounds a week—and not bad pay in those days—who suddenly found himself a popular novelist and a 'made' man, as I considered the meaning of 'made' in those days. All I had to do was to chuck the Leader, go and live where I liked, and sit down and write another one. But the Leader provided me with bread-and-butter, and, although I certainly gave notice of my resignation, I was in no hurry to leave the paper until my royalties began to trickle in. I was so innocent in those days that it never occurred to me to tap the publishers for a bit on account. So, although potentially rich, I was still poor, and carried on in the ordinary way.

White Sunday had been going strong for about two months when, one morning, I was shyly approached by Miss Harding. I just knew her by sight and name. She was a shorthand-typist, one of the chief's secretaries, a neat, dark, shy little thing.

'Mr Harlow,' she said, 'my fiance asked me to speak to you, and offer you his congratulations on the success of your book. He used to be at school with you, and wonders if you would remember him.'

Naturally I asked his name, and she said: 'Thompson.'

'What, old Tommy?' I laughed. 'Well, I'm hanged! I'm awfully glad to hear of him again. Where is he, and what's he doing?'

'He's in a bank,' she said. 'Just now he's living in rooms at Streatham, but as soon as we're married we're going to live at Golders Green.'

'I'd love to see him again,' I said.

'I'll give you his address if you like,' she said, obviously glad to see me so pleased.

She did, too. I made a note of it and lost it immediately afterwards. I was a great deal preoccupied in those days.

'I'll bring you a photograph of him tomorrow,' Miss Harding promised, 'I don't think you'll find he's altered very much. He says he hasn't.'

She was as good as her word, and for once Thompson had told the truth about himself. The photograph was quite a recent one, but I should have recognised it anywhere. The same fat, good-natured face I used to know so well grinned at me from the glazed surface.

'You can keep it, if you like,' said Miss Harding. 'I've got another exactly like it.'

So straight it went into my breast pocket.

They knew at the office that I was only marking time, and the news editor, who was a good fellow, made things as easy for me as he could. About three days later I was sent down to Cornwall on a murder story'. You remember the Penbirro murder? They didn't catch the man until six months afterwards. There wasn't very much story while the affair was still a mystery, and we Pressmen who invaded the village simply ate our heads off and did nothing. Situated as I was, it was an ideal job. I put in about five hours a day on the successor to White Sunday.

And now the really queer part of the story begins. Four miles out of Penbirro is a little place called Glynt, with an old church and a wishing-well, and one or two things worth seeing from an archaeological point of view. That part of the world was strange to me, and I did a bit of exploring by way of recreation. So one afternoon—a scorching June afternoon it was—I walked over to Glynt.

I'd almost reached the village when I stopped by some big iron gates outside a house and immediately had that curious sensation which Pewsey spoke of. I knew that I hadn't been in that part of the world before, and yet I felt that I recognised the house and gardens. But in my case there was an explanation, and I struck it almost at once. I thought I knew it, because Thompson had described it to me so often in the old days.

There was the gabled, Elizabethan house of creeper-clad stone with its shoulder turned to the gate. There were the box trees cut exactly as Thompson had described—the peacock, the hippogriff, the acorn, and the mushroom. And there, in the middle distance, was the raised tennis court enclosed by iron posts and netting. Over the gate was the shield of arms. I knew nothing about heraldry, and I didn't know until later that the freakish bird was supposed to be a raven. Here, to be brief, was the house which Thompson had so often described, complete, so far as I could see, in every detail. He had said that it belonged to his uncle in Hampshire, but here it was in south Cornwall.

Well, my curiosity was fairly roused, and I couldn't help smiling at the thought that Thompson had, for once, been telling something like the truth. That he had erred in the matter of geography simply showed that to tell the exact truth about anything was just outside the compass of his ability. As to whether the place really belonged to his uncle—or had belonged to his uncle—there was only one way to make sure, and that was to go up to the front door and inquire. It was a broiling afternoon, and I was hot and thirsty.

If one of Thompson's relatives really lived there it occurred to me that there might be a welcome for me and a cup of tea. It was a rather queer sort of call to make, but shyness is not one of the failings of your average Pressman. So I pushed open the gate and went up to the front door and rang the bell. Within a few moments the door was opened to me by a smart parlour maid. I inquired for her master and handed her my card.

I stood waiting in the hall while she transferred my card to a salver and turned away. But she hadn't taken two steps when a door opened, and out came a large, greyish man in flannels and an old blazer who looked at me inquiringly. The maid went up to him, offered him my card, and, with that still, small voice peculiar to parlour maids, said: 'This gentleman wishes to see you, sir.'

He took the card, but did not look at it. He looked at me instead. The parlour maid withdrew.

'Yes?' he said. 'What can I do for you?'

I suddenly found myself in rather a tight comer. It took a certain number of words even to begin to explain myself. While I spoke of a school friend who had described the house so minutely and said he used to stay there with his uncle, old Seymour—that turned out to be his name—looked more and more suspicious. Legitimately enough he was plainly wondering what I was leading up to, and he had a blunt direct manner which, I was soon to learn. belied his natural courtesy and kindness of heart.

'Well,' he demanded suddenly, 'what was the name of the boy who said he used to stay here?'

'Thompson,' I replied.

He made the least negative motion with his head.

'Never had a nephew named Thompson,' he said curtly. 'I don't know any Thompsons.'

'Then there must be some mistake,' I said, feeling more unhappy than ever. 'Forgive my asking, but have you been here long?'

'Born here,' he replied, with ominous brevity. He really looked most intensely suspicious, as well he might. I might easily have been a burglar spying out the land. There had been a murder in the district ten days since. I began to make verbal manoeuvres to end what was up till then an unpleasant interview'.

'Well,' I said, laughing uncomfortably, 'I am very sorry to have troubled you. Seeing the house which my friend had described I called in the hope of introducing myself to his people. As your grounds are so distinctive it seems very strange that there should be others like them.'

'Yes,' said Seymour briefly. He was twiddling my card in his fingers, and he glanced at it for the first time. Then his face changed, and he started and stared at me with half a smile.

'Are you Mr Raymond Harlow, the writer?' he asked.

I made a self-deprecatory noise of assent.

'The author of White Sunday?'

I admitted it and began to feel better.

'Yes,' he said, 'I've seen your photograph in the Press. It wasn't a very good one, if I may say so, or I should have recognised you sooner. A most extraordinary coincidence has brought you here, for my wife and daughter and I were all talking about you when you arrived. We have all been reading your book. It's most remarkable that you should have appeared out of the blue in an outlandish place like this just as we were talking about you.'

I explained that I was still a journalist, and that the murder in the next parish had been responsible for bringing me into that part of the world. We both of us began to talk with less restraint, and it ended in his asking me to have a cup of tea. i should find it difficult to make peace with my wife and daughter if I were to let you go without,' he confessed laughing.

Well, you can guess how it was. I was pretty young in those days, and new to my comparative fame. I didn't in the least mind being lionised. So I accompanied him into the drawing-room to meet Mrs Seymour and Eve, who, a year later, was to become my wife.

They were the kindest people in the world, with quick instincts for making friends. They flattered me outrageously, but their flattery appealed to something more than my baser instincts, because their liking for While Sunday was so obviously sincere. Within a very short time we were all laughing heartily at the extraordinary chance which had brought me to their house. They pressed me to stay to dinner, and over dinner I told the story of Thompson, and how he used to describe the gardens and the outside of the very house they were living in. We hit on what we thought was an obvious explanation. Thompson as a boy had been down that way on a holiday, had seen the house and been attracted by it, and the rest, after that, was entirely typical of Thompson.

After dinner we all went for a stroll in the gardens.

'We shan't see our ghost,' said Eve, slipping her hand inside her father's arm, 'because it's too early for him.'

'You've got a ghost, then?' I asked.

'Oh, yes!' said Seymour, so lightly that he might have been joking.

'We've got the most peculiar ghost in the world. Unlike any other sort of ghost, this one gets older. We've watched him grow up from a boy into a man.'

They all laughed, and Eve hastily added:

'Oh, yes, it's quite true! We've all seen him several times. We saw him first as a boy years ago, and, as father says, he's a man now. And he stays outside—he never comes into the house. This has been going on nearly ever since I can remember. He's quite pleasant for a ghost, but I do wish we knew what he wants.'

I don't know what made me do it, but something prompted me to pull Thompson's photograph out of my breast pocket.

'I suppose,' I said, 'this isn't your ghost, is it?'

They gathered around me to look, and immediately there was a shout of surprise from Seymour, and faint screams from Mrs Seymour and Eve. The ghost had been identified.

I hung on down at Penbirro as long as I could, but I was recalled at last. You may guess how anxious I was to meet Thompson. I had lost his address, but I knew I could always get it again from Miss Harding.

I've told you there were reasons why I haven't turned this into a short story. Coincidences are almost taboo, but in the freakish way things happen in real life, I ran into Thompson quite accidentally almost immediately on my return. I received my first cheque for royalties, a nice fat one, and bore it proudly off to the Temple Bar branch of the London and Suburban Bank to open an account there. I was just coming out of the manager's office when I spotted Thompson sitting at one of the desks in the body of the kirk, so to speak. He spotted me, too, and came over to the counter to speak, grinning all over his fat face. It was neither the time nor the place for a heart-to-heart talk, so I made a luncheon appointment with him. An hour or so later we were facing each other over a small table in Romano's, talking about old times. I went very warily to work with him.

'Well, Tommy,' I said, when we had exhausted each other's stock of O.H. news, 'do you still entertain your friends with little stories about yourself?'

He laughed and coloured.

'Oh, you needn't remind me of that,' he said. 'I'm a reformed character now. When I die I shall be able to walk arm-in-arm with the shade of George Washington. My object was solely to entertain, and I brightened many a young life.'

'I've never forgotten,' I said, 'about your uncle's house.'

He laughed uneasily. Plainly he thought I was taking advantage of his past failings.

'Well,' he returned, 'at least I didn't invent that. Well, not exactly.'

'Tommy,' I said, 'be plain with me.'

'I don't know that I can. As a matter of fact, I dreamed that house. I've been dreaming it all my life. I still go there in my dreams and roam about the gardens. I don't suppose there is any such place, and certainly no uncle of mine ever lived in it, if it does exist, but I didn't exactly invent it. Queer things, dreams, aren't they?'

But evidently he didn't yet know how queer dreams could be.

'Tommy,' I said suddenly, 'have you ever been to Cornwall at any period of your life?'

He shook his head.

'Will you swear that you haven't?'

He looked puzzled, but he gave the required oath seriously enough.

'Did any of your people ever come from that part of the world?'

'No; my father came of an Essex family, and my mother was Scotch. What makes you ask?'

After a little I told him what made me ask.

And there (said Harlow) the story ends; and you'll see why I haven't made use of it. According to all the canons of fiction we should have discovered that Thompson was related to the Seymours, or that Glynt House had once belonged to his people. And, moreover, Thompson, and not I, ought to have married Eve. From the story point of view it's hopelessly unsatisfactory.

We went into the matter most exhaustively. There was no point where we could discover that the respective family trees of the Thompsons and the Seymours touched branches. There was no reason at all that we could discover why Glynt House should have attracted Thompson. He had never seen it nor heard of it, yet he had dreamed of it, and sometimes while he slept his spirit had wandered free among its gardens. It is all quite inexplicable, and I think it is likely so to remain.

There is only one more curious point. A year or so later Thompson accompanied me down to stay with the Seymours, and saw for the first time the place of which he had dreamed and which he had actually 'haunted'. After that the 'hauntings' ceased. The Seymours are still living there, but they never see him now.

The Frontier of Dreams

Amongst the scattered remains of an earthwork that had once concealed a battery, lay half-a-score of artillerymen, splashed by shrapnel. Nine of them were dead. Darrell, a junior subaltern, was still alive. Night had silenced the guns, and the ambulance men were abroad on their work of mercy, but as yet Darrell lay undiscovered.

For long hours he had lain there. He had no knowledge of the extent of his hurt, and knew only the dire torment of moving and the worse torment of lying still. Delirium had overtaken him long since, and saved him from wondering whether he were to live or die.

In occasional lucid moments he looked towards death as a tired traveller watches for the lights of home.

It had been a nightmare day, and the night had brought no change for the better. The firing had at least rendered the wounded inaudible. Now their voices went up to the heavens, a dreadful protest against the folly and cruelty of men. Darrell had contrived to keep silent. Wounded officers had been asked to make as little noise as possible.

He lay motionless now, without the strength or will to move. Away to the left was a little wood, wherein the owls were calling. These sounds, low, persistent, mournful, awoke in him a vague consciousness. He had heard them often before. Back in England long years ago, a little boy had often lain awake in a blue and white nursery listening to the owls in the plantation beyond the garden. For a moment he was back again in the little room, gazing at a dim blue square of the sky framed by the window and thinly veiled by the lace curtains. He had a dim vision of Dobbin, his gallant wooden charger, and of the piled boxes in which many leaden battalions lay sleeping. Then he realised that himself and the little boy were far removed; that a whole lifetime divided them. He felt the damp earth beneath the palm of his hand.

It seemed to him that a motionless star, peering down through a rift in the clouds, was God's eye watching him, and silently speaking a message of peace. And at the message, pain fell away from him like a loosened garment. With the passing of pain, there came to him a blessed forgetfulness. It made the shattered man whole and set him on a horse, and lo! he was riding with his troops through London streets, between pavements lined with cheering crowds and windows gay with flags and fluttering handkerchiefs.

Then, when the scene changed suddenly he did not think it strange. He accepted the change with the calm philosophy of one who dreams. He was younger, and it was a spring morning. He knew that it was spring before he noticed that the fruit trees were pink and white with blossom and the hedges a tender green, because he could feel it in his blood.

He knew the road as a man knows his mother's face. The hedge on his left hand fringed a long narrow orchard, and was protected by barbed wire on the inside because the boys wrought terrible havoc among Farmer Martin's cherries. The hedge ended close to a high red wall, with moss growing on the mortar between the bricks, and he knew that presently he would pass a great wrought-iron gate with a lamp at the top overhanging the road. He had forgotten who lived in the big house, and made no effort to remember, since it did not concern him. Another half-mile, and the road would sink down into a pretty valley where the church stood, with the vicarage nestling close against it for company. His thoughts were centred on the vicarage because Mavis lived there.

He had forgotten that Mavis, as she grew up, had treated him more coldly year by year, that the little girl who loved the boy had grown into the young woman who scarcely tolerated the man. Sometimes he had thought that she was only dissembling her old love of him, but he had never gathered the courage to ask her, and he never knew. One day, when the old vicarage was even quieter than usual, and the blinds were drawn, he had kissed Mavis for the first time since she was a child. Her face was cold and white and his tears had soiled it. . . . Afterwards they had carried her out and hidden her under the ground, within sight of her own little window. But Darrell had forgotten all this. His dream was very merciful.

He walked with the buoyant step of youth, and his footfalls on the road beat time to the tune of a song. At length he stood before the front door of the vicarage, and presently old Martha, the servant, looking as ludicrous as ever in the little cap that always sat upright on her iron-grey hair, stood framed in the doorway. Looking past her he could see the 'Ecce Homo' picture overhanging the stairs, the antlers over the dining-room door, the familiar hats hanging on pegs in the stand. One of Mavis's garden hats was there, the one trimmed with cherries.

No, Miss Mavis was not at home, but he would know where to find her. Having so delivered herself, old Martha closed the door. Very strange conduct on the part of old Martha! What could she mean? He turned away pondering.

He found himself in the churchyard, where the mounds were very green and old tombstones reared themselves out of the ground at crazy angles. Then he laughed softly to himself. This was not the place to look for Mavis. But where could she be?

The memory of a little maid of ten, playing by a stream in the copse, came back to him. She had damped her feet and had taken off her shoes and stockings to dry them in the sun, not daring to go home bearing the signs of her naughtiness. He had found her there and taught her how to play at robbers. Of course, that happened years and years ago, and he could not expect to find her there now. But he went to the copse to look for her all the same. One does these things in dreams.

He heard the murmur of a little stream, and, leaving the path, pushed his way through the undergrowth until he came to a clearing, where the sun shone down upon a glorious garden of forest flowers, and made diamonds on the surface of the hurrying brook. The woods around looked very deep and cool. Two little shoes disgracefully muddy, and a pair of damp stockings, lay in the sun by the stump of a felled tree. He stooped to pick them up, and as he did so his name was called, and he heard a laugh, very sweet and musical.

He straightened himself and looked about him.

'Mavis,' he called, 'where are you?'

She came out from behind a tree and ran towards him. He gazed on her in a kind of foolish wonder, surprised at seeing a little child. He bent down and her lips trembled on his cheek.

'I thought you were a big, grown-up girl,' he faltered.

She shook her head, smiling, with a gesture that tossed back a wealth of rebellious curls.

'No, no,' she said, 'you are thinking of another Mavis!'

For a moment he did not understand. His memory was guarded by a locked door, but for a brief moment the shadow of grim reality fumbled with the key.

'You are to come with me, dear,' she whispered. I am going to take you where you will be happy.'

The child's fingers closed on his hands. The dream passed, but he did not wake.

A man bearing a lantern stumbled over the broken ground, and, bending, drew his breath with a little hissing noise. Without moving, he called to a small crowd of ambulance men who followed, ghostlike and silent.

'There's about a dozen more here,' he said in a muffled voice. 'One officer.'

The sound of a low voice asking a question preceded the others as they drew nearer.

The first-comer shook his head.

'No,' he answered, 'all dead.'

The Mystery of the Sealed Garret

Punctually at ten o'clock—for the new policeman was not yet to be trusted—Billy Chignell went through his nightly ritual of crying 'Time, gentlemen!' in tones ranged between brisk joviality and reluctant severity. When he had ushered the last customer out into the night he put up the heavy bar and walked upstairs into the smoke-room.

He had four 'guests' sleeping under his roof that night, which, considering that the time of the year was early spring, was something approaching a record. Few visitors came to St Fay, save in the summer, and most of those preferred the charms of the great new hotel, with its 'desirable situation' on the headland near the golf course. Most of the men who came to spend a night at the Schooner Inn were commercial travellers, and two or three in the course of a week was about the average number. Now chance had brought three all at once, and besides these there was Mr Dimsdale, who had been there a fortnight. Mr Dimsdale was a leisured, cultured, and extremely pleasant person in the late thirties, who cherished a delusion that there were trout in the upper reaches of the St Fay river, and spent his days trying to catch them.

Billy Chignell, good sociable soul, liked nothing better than a glass and a chat in the smoke-room after hours with anybody who might be staying in the house.

He entered unobtrusively and sat himself on a chair near the door, for the four were engaged upon a discussion which had already waxed hot. Dimsdale, vaguely suspected by Billy Chignell of being a scholar and authority on most things, sat on a horsehair chair with an elbow resting on the table. His lips were set in a faint smile, which the landlord interpreted as a sign of suppressed amusement. Walters, a serious little man, who was something of a mystic and compelled by hard fate to vend frivolous articles beloved by womenfolk, sat simmering in a mild rage. Beside him, but a little to the rear, sat Dorley, the representative of a firm of wholesale haberdashers, smirking openly. He loved to see Walters under the lash of another's tongue, but lacked the wits himself to administer the lash. Chudd, who travelled for a firm of brush manufacturers, sat in the largest armchair and laid down the law with all the vigour of a man who relies upon noise and persistence in an argument rather than upon his own reasoning powers.

'It makes me sick,' he was saying—'right down sick, it does. How ever children, let alone grown men and women, can believe such fiddle-faddle beats me. Everybody who believes in Spiritualism ought to be in a lunatic asylum, and those who go about trying to kid other people ought to get two years' hard for it. That's what I say, and I don't care who hears me say it. Ghosts—spirits—bah!'

He was a big man was Mr Chudd, with a very red face and neck. For the rest he was a blatant self-opinionated person, with hardly sufficient bovine intelligence to be aware that he was a bully.

The situation was perfectly clear to Billy Chignell before he had been ten seconds in the room. Little Walters, in the hope of starting some quiet and amicable discussion, had remarked how much talk of Spiritualism one heard nowadays, and ventured his opinion that 'there might be something in it'.

This had brought Chudd down upon him like a hundredweight of bricks, and he had proceeded to dispose of the denizens of the spirit world, using heavy sarcasm alternately with his table-thumping methods of reasoning. Dorley, with nods and half-words of encouragement, had egged him on, and Walters was having very much the worse of it, because Chudd, having much the louder voice, would not allow him to speak. Dimsdale was sitting quiet and saying nothing.

Billy Chignell disliked Chudd, who was noisy and would not brook the opinion which did not exactly coincide with his own. He did not think highly of Chudd's intelligence. For one thing, Chudd did not come from London—only from Bristol—and he was therefore not entitled to speak with the voice of authority.

Billy Chignell was a little disappointed to find that Chudd held the same views as himself. Not being a lawyer, he was unable to argue successfully against his own beliefs. He was, however, tolerant on the subject. If people wanted to believe in ghosts and such-like—well, they were welcome. One of his rooms was supposed to be haunted, and the stories which had reached his ears were strange and disturbing. He was inclined, lazily, to suppose that there must be some quite simple and natural explanation. He did not believe in ghosts, but he doubted his own courage, and so he had taken the line of least resistance and shut up the room. It was hardly ever needed.

'I've only just come in,' he remarked, 'but I'll lay Mr Chudd's been weighing in with some mighty heavy arguments against ghosts and spirits. I don't suppose any'll dare show themselves now.'

The delicate shaft of sarcasm glanced off the thick skin of the bagman. Dimsdale, the angler, however, took advantage of the pause to enter into the discussion.

'Mr Chudd,' he said, 'hasn't favoured us with any arguments. We have heard him bang the table and shout and behave offensively, but no gems of reason have fallen from his lips. He has said Rubbish, and Bosh, and Nonsense, all of which are emphatic as an opinion, but unconvincing as an argument.'

Billy Chignell grinned delightedly, thankful that Chudd had found an antagonist who could take his measurements. Little Walters laughed and plucked up the courage to say:

'Yes, saying Rubbish and Bosh don't prove anything, Mr Chudd.'

Chudd's face flamed redder than ever. He was the natural enemy of men of Dimsdale's type. He conceived his intelligence to be the greater, but he had not what he called 'the gift of the gab'.

'Proof!' he cried, 'It don't want proof. If you said that two and two made five instead of four, it 'ud be rot, but nobody could prove it was rot, except by their own common-sense.'

'Oh, I see—that's the difficulty.' Dimsdale's voice was as smooth as milk. 'You are going by your own common-sense. But surely you don't expect other men to rely on your reasoning as an infallible guide. For instance, one of our leading scientists, one of the cleverest men in the land, is a confirmed believer in the things your intelligence puts to scorn. You may be a cleverer man, but I never heard of you before I met you, and if I had to pin my faith to one or the other of you I could not pin it to you.'

His speech ended in a mild uproar. Little Walters was bouncing about on his chair. Dorley, who observed that a greater man than Chudd was in the field, shamelessly changed sides and joined in the laughter. Chudd struggled to make his voice heard above the din, but for once in a way it was he who was shouted down.

'Yes,' he cried, as soon as he could make himself heard, 'and that man's as mad as a hatter.'

'Because he disagrees with you?'

'No, because he—he—everybody knows he's mad.'

Dimsdale shook his head slowly and regretfully.

'No,' he said, 'you have talked for a long time and been very rude, but nothing in the shape of legitimate argument has crossed your lips. Everybody does not believe—much less know—that that distinguished gentleman is mad. I am sure he is not. He may be a self-deceiver, but that again requires proof. You don't believe in a spirit-world partly because you think it beneath your dignity as a sober, hard-headed man of business to inquire into anything that sounds to you so childish. You don't want to believe in such things.'

'And half the people who do believe only believe because they want to. All the people who say they've seen ghosts, or talked with the dead, are liars—those that aren't mad.'

Dimsdale smiled.

'Yes,' he said, 'I'm afraid the worst enemy to the Spiritualist is the liar. There are a lot of people going about who say they've seen ghosts, when they don't even imagine they have. They believe in such things and they want to convince other people. It may happen though that certain pig-headed people have had strange experiences which they won't talk about because they don't want to believe. Seeing isn't believing to a pig-headed man.'

Chudd sat upright and leaned a little forward.

'Do you believe in ghosts?' he challenged.

Nailed down by a direct question, Dimsdale smiled and shook his head.

'No'

'Well, then, there you are.'

'Not at all. I don't disbelieve either. As a cautious man I take the middle course. I'm not anxious to be convinced. There's a room in this house that's supposed to be haunted, but I haven't plagued Mr Chignell to let me sleep in it.'

'A haunted room? In this house?'

Dorley and Walters repeated the words, and all eyes were turned upon the landlord.

'No there aren't,' he muttered. 'Aren't no such things.'

'Of course there ain't!' Chudd cried. 'Which room is it, boss?'

'Not the one where the murder happened?' Dorley inquired, 'It's shut up now,' said Chignell. 'I don't believe in ghosts, but there are folks who do, and I've got my living to make.'

'Did anybody see anything there?' Dimsdale asked,

'I dunno—there was complaints.'

'Complaints? What of?'

'Oh, all sorts of things. All imagination, I dare say. But there was complaints, so I shut it up. I can't afford to have people complaining in my house.'

'What's this about a murder?' Walters inquired eagerly, 'I didn't know there'd been one here.'

'It was some years back, just before I took the house,' Billy Chignell explained. 'A skipper it was. He'd just come ashore and he took a bed here for the night. It seems he'd had trouble with some of his crew—lascars and black men and such-like. Anyhow, he was found dead in bed in the morning—strangled! They never caught the man.'

'He must have been in this house the whole time,' Dorley exclaimed.

'No; they reckoned he'd managed to hide himself in The Black Horse, opposite, and crawled across from one window to the other. With the streets narrow, like they are here, and the upper storeys nearly meeting overhead, anybody could do it. The skipper had locked his door overnight, and it was found locked in the morning.'

'P'r'aps Mr Chudd 'ud like to spend the night there,' said Walters, grinning.

'I wouldn't mind.'

'No,' said Chignell. 'I don't want any complaints.'

'I shan't make any complaints.'

'I think Mr Chudd should certainly sleep there if he wishes,' Dimsdale put in. 'I wouldn't myself, because I don't disbelieve in ghosts.'

'Afraid!' said Chudd.

'Not necessarily. I don't go about in search of danger and discomfort, that is all. But you, as you definitely disbelieve, have nothing to fear.'

He looked sharply at Billy Chignell, who was preparing to utter a protest.

'I hate suggesting that our worthy host should be put to any trouble,' he continued, 'but it would be a matter of only a few minutes to have bedding put in that room. And if Mr Chudd is really anxious'

'I am,' said Chudd, and he meant it.

The man was honest enough. He was quite convinced that he had nothing worse than a damp bed to fear. Give him a dry bed and he would be all right. Billy Chignell hesitated. He had had complaints about the room, but he did not believe that it was haunted. He could not see of what advantage it would be to give Chudd the opportunity of crowing like a gamecock over the breakfast-table and pouring fresh scorn on the credulity of weaker mortals.

However, it was obvious that Dimsdale wished it. Dimsdale was watching him now, anxiously, appealingly. He found it hard to deny Dimsdale anything.

'All right,' he said, 'you can sleep there if you want, Mr Chudd. Only you won't forget I did warn you that people have made complaints about that room.'

The room of evil repute assigned to Chudd proved to be a cheerless and damp-smelling garret. It was in the old part of the house, which means that portion which had escaped the hands of a previous owner with a passion for renovation and reconstruction. The floor was on a slant and the ceiling hung absurdly low—so low that a tall man had to remember to bend his head as he passed under the long beam on his way to the dressing-table.

The one window faced another window in the house opposite, and the two were so near together that, by leaning well out, one could easily touch the outer sill of this opposite window. The thoroughfare below was so narrow that an automobile could hardly squeeze through, and the upper storeys of both houses projected, after the picturesque fashion of mediaeval architecture.

Chudd held this to account for the air of depression—something more than that of mere desuetude—which seemed present in the room. It had never had, from year's end to year's end, one glimpse of the sun. The house opposite shut it out as completely as if no window were there at all. No wonder nervous and imaginative people had suffered in such a room. He whistled as he undressed in order to convince himself that he was no nervous mouse of a man. But he did not whistle long, because the atmosphere of the room seemed unresponsive. This feeling he found difficult to analyse. It was a little as if he had made questionable jokes in a company which declined to be amused and eyed him coldly. There was no company present in this case, but he seemed to have aroused some chilly and baleful consciousness.

'It's like singing comic songs in a vault,' he reflected, a little while after he had ceased whistling. 'A chap doesn't want to believe in ghosts to get the horrors in this room. If the sunlight could only get in'

To do him justice, he was perfectly unafraid. He was barely conscious of the slight weakening of his nerves—a mere nothing. He put down that, such as it was, to the brief story of the murder. Ugh! Easy to imagine a murder happening there. His mind, slightly more alert and imaginative than usual, conjured up an ugly picture of the sleeping captain, lying on the very bed which he was about to enter, and some ugly shape, which had come out of the night, bending over him and crushing his throat with hooked, claw-like Fingers.

Before getting into bed he closed the lattice window, although ordinarily he was a great believer in the virtues of fresh air. He told himself that the room was already cold enough, and that the draught between the chimney and the door was sufficient to keep the room healthy. At the back of his mind he could not help remembering that it was through that same open window that the assassin had crept to strangle a man lying there where he was going to lie.

The room was very dark when he had blown out the candle. The house opposite which shut out the sun by day, shut out all but a fitful glimmer of the dim moonlight. He looked long and intently, but could not see the window clearly, only a faint dimness which grew slowly beyond the posts at the foot of the bed.

'If anybody tries any tricks with me,' he thought savagely, clenching a great fist beneath the bedclothes, 'I'll smash 'em!'

It somehow comforted him to remind himself of his strength and manhood, although he would have denied that he stood in need of comfort. Three or four long minutes he lay, trying to define the shape of the window; then he turned over and lay on his side and tried to compose himself to sleep.

But that night sleep, which was usually so responsive to his wooing, played the jade with him and mocked him from a distance. He turned from side to side, restless and out of temper, and continued to toss and turn until -

Quite how it began he did not know. Perhaps it was no more than a creaking board which began that unreasonable nervousness which seemed to grow in him as quickly as the mango tree of the Indian juggler. Somewhere in the room a board did creak. There was nothing unusual in that, of course, and a hundred causes might have been assigned to it. Chudd, however, could not think of one. Lying there in the dark it did not seem right to him that a board should creak unless somebody trod on it. No, no; he wasn't afraid, only—only what made it creak?

He turned over in bed, and the board creaked again, as if in response to his movement. The breath he drew tingled and felt cold in his nostrils. His eyes were closed, and he had to summon resolution before he could open them. Perhaps the captain had heard that board creak -

His open eyes encountered nothing but the empty darkness and he breathed relief. Deciding that he must force himself somehow to go to sleep, he turned over once more. The board creaked again. This time he felt his heart beating, and one ear, pressed against the pillow, heard the loud, quick drumming of an artery. Damn that creaking board! If that wasn't enough to give a man the horrors, what was? It was as if there were somebody in the room—somebody who turned to look at him every time he moved on the bed. An unpleasant thought, that! To himself he fiercely denied that he was nervous, but he did not move, although he wanted to turn over again. Also, it was entirely his own affair if he chose to breathe more gently; it did not mean that he was afraid of attracting the attention of anything that might be taking cover in the darkness. Besides, there was nothing there.

He lay still until the posture tortured him; then he turned again. This time the board did not creak, but its not doing so, perversely enough, increased his discomfort. It seemed to prove that it was not his movement on the bed causing a slight pressure on the boards which had made the sound. He drew a long breath, and the board creaked again then, as if the sound of breathing had attracted unwelcome attention.

Chudd became conscious of feeling slightly damp. In the stillness he fancied he could hear something—something more than the blood singing in his veins. It sounded like a chorus of voices singing—a very long way off, low, but terribly distinct. All imagination he knew, but - He clenched his hands. He could not now disguise from himself the fact that he, Alfred Chudd, was nerve-ridden and afraid, and for no reason that the Alfred Chudd of normal times would accept for a reason. The breath came from his lips in a thin trickle of vapour, as if he released it grudgingly.

He lay and sweated, feebly battling against the invading waves of horror, and too engrossed in staving off a nightmare panic to curse himself for owning the weakness, which he had despised in other men. It was not merely the creaking of a board which had brought him to these straits, but because he was conscious—although not through the medium of any sense that he could name—of the presence of some horror, a vague, nameless beastliness for which there was no description in any human language.

Heavens! What was that! His heart bounded within him like a live thing, and every nerve in his body made for him a separate agony. That was no piece of imagination—that noise, that movement at the far end of the room. While his pulses still raced, he realised the meaning of the sound. The window had opened and was swinging in the night breeze that moaned along the narrow streets.

The window had opened! Yes, and when he had shut it before getting into bed he tried its firmness and been satisfied. It had taken pounds of pressure to shift it, but it had shifted. A strong draught invaded the room and breathing over his pillowed head cooled the sweat in his hair. The window had opened as—O God of pity!—as it had opened that night the captain -

No, no, he wouldn't, he daren't think about that.

The seconds lagged and became periods of eternity. He knew that his normal self would have risen and closed the window, but he dared not move.

The least movement—even of a hand or limb beneath the bedclothes—seemed to attack the resentful gaze of countless unseen eyes out there in the darkness. If he got out of bed, surely they would all come clamouring around him.

In the midst of all the stealthy restlessness that seemed to be going on in the room, his hearing—or some other sense—made him aware of some other sound or movement that was definite and purposeful. Someone—something —was creeping towards him from the direction of the open window, slinking, huddled and crouched, along the carpet. Chudd was now wet through with sweat. He felt his hair stiffen and rise.

'This is a nightmare,' he told himself; but in a nightmare one cannot move, and Chudd was able, only he dared not.

But the climax was yet to come, and it came along moments later when something cold touched his cheeks and deftly and gently felt its way down to his windpipe. His tortured brain knew it to be a clammy hand with long bony fingers. They fastened on to his throat and broke the spell which had kept him lying still as a felled log. With his ecstasy of terror came the fighting courage of the cornered rat.

He uttered a harsh, gurgling cry as the fingers tightened on his windpipe in an agonising grip. As he writhed beneath it the strength of ten came to his aid. He lunged out, grunting with the effort, great smashing blows which struck the empty air. He tore the hands from his throat, and, with a snarling scream, struck again and again. Half rising, he lashed out like a madman, and toppled off the bed on to the floor in a huddle of bedclothes. His head struck the handle of the door as he picked himself up, and a moment later he had flung it open and half tripped, half staggered across the landing, trailing blankets and sheets behind him.

There was a horsehair sofa in the coffee-room; there was also an oil lamp which might be lit. He made his way there, and remained with a light burning until dawn was in the sky.

Alfred Chudd's appearance was such as to attract attention when, rather late, he made his appearance at the breakfast table. He looked pale and hollow-eyed and worse tempered than usual, and he kept his chin well down over his collar. Billy Chignell was in the room as he entered, the landlord having just brought in a fresh supply of bread-and-butter for the three already seated.

'Good morning, Mr Chudd,' he said, turning half round. 'I hope you slept all right.'

Chudd grunted an affirmative.

'No complaints about the room, I hope?'

Chudd, although not looking directly at them, was aware of four pairs of challenging eyes focused upon his face. He hesitated only for a moment.

Now that the sun was shining into the coffee-room it was possible to conceive himself to have been the victim of a nightmare. Besides, the humiliation of telling his story was something not to be borne.

'No complaints,' he grunted.

'What?' exclaimed Dorley. 'You haven't seen the ghost?'

'Ghost be hanged!' exclaimed Chudd, in quite his old manner, if I'd been a madman or a liar I might have seen fifty. But I knew nothing would happen in that room, and nothing did happen. Pity I'm moving on to Bodmin today, or I'd sleep in it again and welcome.'

It did him good to talk in that vein, and as he continued the breakfast-table shook beneath his fist, and the room became highly uncomfortable for Mr Walters.

Dimsdale, who had been the first to come down to breakfast, was the first to leave the table. He went downstairs and into the outhouse at the back where he kept his rod ready jointed and his creel and tackle. Some march browns needed tying, and he came out into the light to thread the 'points'. Billy Chignell, emerging from the back door to shake a mat, saw him, dropped the mat, and made towards him. He was doing his best to grin and look severe at the same time, and his round, jolly face was oddly distorted in the effort.

'Doesn't it beat cock-fighting?' he asked, in a hoarse whisper. 'There's that there Chudd, he won't eat his words and he looks nearer dead than alive. He's had an awful night, and he won't say a word. If he doesn't believe in ghosts now'

'I rather gathered from his shouting,' said Dimsdale, wetting the end of a point and holding a little brown fly up to the light, 'that he was still rather more than sceptical.'

The landlord's voice became a thought more serious. There was a note of respectful rebuke in the tone of it.

'Oh, Mr Dimsdale,' he said, 'it's been a rare lark. But you shouldn't have done it.'

'Done what? Dash it, my sight's getting very bad, or I'm very clumsy this morning.'

'Come now, Mr Dimsdale, sir, it must have been you. Dorley and Walters wouldn't have dared. It beats me how you knew what the others complained of, for I know I didn't tell you. But I could tell what had happened to Chudd, although he did keep his chin well down. I could see the marks on his throat—bruises—all black and blue.'

Dimsdale lowered the fly and stared at Billy Chignell.

'Are you suggesting,' he asked, half laughing, 'that I went to that fellow's room last night and nearly throttled him?'

'I don't suppose you meant to nearly throttle him. But he won't forget it in a hurry.'

Dimsdale gazed at him in blank amazement.

'Well,' he said, i swear I never went near his room.'

Billy Chignell stared harder than ever.

'And I swear I didn't,' he said, 'and I'll take my solemn dying oath that Walters and Dorley didn't.'

They continued to stare at one another. The sunlight was very bright and warm and seemed to deny what was in their minds.

'The others,' said Billy Chignell, sinking his voice, 'all complained of the same thing. Somebody came in the night and tried to choke 'em, so they said. I didn't believe it, and I'm not going to say that I believe it now.'

'Nor am I,' said Dimsdale, and added, after a pause: 'Well, what are you going to do about it?'

'Do about it? I'm a plain man and I don't believe in ghosts or haunted rooms, and I don't want to. But I've got my living to get, and I can't afford to have people making complaints in my house, so I'm going to shut that room up again right away, and people can go down on their knees before I let them sleep in it again. As a plain man who doesn't pretend to understand some things—and doesn't want to—don't you think I'm right?'

'As another plain man,' Dimsdale answered. 'I'm rather inclined to think you are.'

'I'm Sure It Was No. 31'

It happened many years ago when I was a boy of eighteen, out house-hunting for my mother in a London suburb within a mile and a half of where we were then living. There were many houses to be let in those happy Edwardian days, and, having a bicycle and knowing my mother's requirements, I could thus save her fruitless journeys to some which I knew she would not consider. I had in my pocket several 'orders to view' from local agents, and was on my way to an address when the strangest incident of my life befell me. It was on a sunny October afternoon, and, apart from feeling lethargic and depressed, I believe I was in a normal state of health.

My way took me along a tram-route, and all the side-roads on my left were culs-de-sac, ending at the boundary wall of a great park. I looked down all these side-roads as I passed, and suddenly I stopped at a comer and got off my machine—for I had seen a 'to let' board slanting over some railings about halfway down on the right.

It was a road of small villas, just suitable for our purpose, and the board belonged to agents with whom we were already in touch. Then—although I could find no house in that road on my list—I decided to go and investigate. So I rose up, balanced my machine against the kerb, and rang.

I was quite unprepared for the sight of the lady who came to the door.

She seemed old to my young eyes, although I daresay she was under forty, and I forget how she was dressed, but instinct told me at a glance that she was out of her proper setting in that shabby little house.

Well, I uncovered, explained my errand, and apologised for having no order to view. At the same time I offered to show her other 'orders' from the same agent.

'Oh,' she said, 'I'm sorry. The men ought to have taken the board away. I've decided to stay on.'

I think she recognised me—as already I had recognised her—as someone who had seen better days. I was a shabby, untidy, lank-haired, sallow boy, not at all of the type to interest a heart-hungry widow. Probably I looked jaded and tired. Whatever the reason, she said:

'Won't you come in and have a cup of tea?'

She was just like some other fellow's mater in the days before poverty had changed my environment, and all my shyness went from me on the instant. I followed her into the front room, where two surprises awaited me. The lesser of these was the furniture—much too massive for its setting—and the oil paintings of Army and Navy officers of past generations.

The greater surprise was the girl of about sixteen who rose to greet me as her mother said: 'This is my daughter. Mumps, darling, I don't yet know this gentleman's name'

I daresay I was still staring as I supplied it. She was about the most vivid and striking young person I had ever seen, with long black hair hanging loose over her shoulders and a wonderful warm complexion which seemed to light the room for me. Chocolate-box prettiness? Well, perhaps it was, but it reduced me for a time to bashful nervousness.

Well, we sat talking for a while and my hostess succeeded in overcoming my shyness by talking about herself. Her name was Ellis, and I gathered that she was a widow. Invariably she addressed her daughter as Mumps, and I never knew the girl's Christian name.

Presently I noticed on one of the walls an oil painting of 'Mumps' done apparently a year or two before. It looked a little amateurish beside the others, and I was not surprised to hear that it was Mrs Ellis's own work. 'Oh, Mumps is a much better artist than I am,' she laughed. 'Show him some of your drawings, dear, while I get tea.'

'Mumps' had little to say for herself and seemed as shy as her new acquaintance. But she unearthed a portfolio and increased my embarrassment by showing some figure-drawings which struck me as being extremely well done but rather startling. However, she displayed them in the same manner in which she might have shown me views of a cathedral.

Had I been older and more experienced I might have jumped to a certain conclusion about that mother and daughter, and I am sure that I should have been wrong. Whatever the mother may have done—and I suspect nothing worse than unpaid bills—there was nothing coarse about her. Besides, a shabby boy with only coppers in his pocket was hardly fair game for harpies. Over tea I told them about myself. I wonder if they really believed that I had been—and probably still was—the youngest professional writer in the world, and that I had had a story accepted a year before while I was still at school. I had to own, though, that I had no work at the time.

But even if Mrs Ellis took me for a young liar I was well aware that she liked me, and it did not account for her very strange behaviour when I came to go.

She had told me little about herself save that she was a widow, but she mentioned one of her relatives when I told her about my father's fatal illness—which had left me a schoolboy of seventeen with a penniless mother to support.

'What a pity,' she said, 'that he didn't see my uncle,' And she named a knighted physician in Harley Street.

Well, I could not stay for ever and the time came for me to go. 'Mumps' and her mother preceded me into the little hall, and I took leave first of the girl. Mrs Ellis opened the door and I said goodbye to her on the step.

Of course, I had been hoping that she would ask me to come again, but she did not. Her manner, despite her self-possession, was in the circumstances extraordinary. She seemed almost tearful and might have been parting for ever from an old and dear friend. For I knew that she liked me, just as I knew that she knew I had fallen in love with 'Mumps'. Had I done the incredible in bending over and kissing her, I know she would have given me a little hug. And a moment later she would have closed the door softly upon me for ever.

Why? I do not know. It all seemed very strange. But I was yet to realise how extraordinary had been the events of that afternoon.

Of course I remembered Mrs Ellis's address. The road was marked by a comer shop—I bought cigarettes there on my way home—and the number 31 was easily memorised as the reverse of the unlucky 13.

During the following day—and indeed for many days—I could not get the girl out of my head. She baulked my efforts to write cheap fiction. I felt that I must see her again or go mad.

It did not seem so difficult, for a short cycle ride brought me to the corner of her road. Even if she still went to school—and my impression was that she did not—there was always the chance of meeting her mother out shopping and getting a casual invitation to tea.

For hours at a time, mornings and afternoons, I haunted the main street of that other suburb during the next fortnight, and haunted it in vain. Passing and re-passing the top of the road I could catch no glimpse of either lady, but saw, as I had expected, that the estate agent's board was gone.

At the end of the fortnight I decided in desperation to make an uninvited call, timing myself to arrive at tea-time. My excuse? Oh, I could tell Mrs Ellis that we had not yet found a suitable house and ask if she had heard of one. She would see through me, of course, but I could not help it. I knew I ought to keep away, but I went—to desolation and bewilderment.

I thought at first it was a charwoman who came to the door, although I could see that the furniture in the hall had changed—and not for the better—since my other visit.

'Mrs Ellis?' said the woman, shaking her head. 'No, I don't know the name around here, and we've been here nearly two years.'

I apologised and bolted. After all, I must have made a mistake in the number. But I was sure of the road, because it was marked by the corner shop, and the man would know. I went in and bought a packet of cigarettes and it was the same man who served me again. He gave me a strange look.

'Mrs Ellis? Well, she used to live at No. 31, but she's been gone about two years now.'

Then, probably mistaking the look on my face, he added: 'A lot of people would like to know what became of her.'

The innuendo was obvious. A moonlight flit, and money owed all round. Yes, but I'd had tea with her in that house a fortnight before. There was a silly mistake somewhere.

But the man described her and 'Mumps', even mentioning the silly nickname. Further, he knew about the Harley Street doctor.

'Yes,' he said, 'she was a well-connected lady. I wonder where she went. It's a long time now. Your guvnor's going to have a job to find her.'

I was too shocked and dazed to resent being taken for a debt-collector's spy. All I realised was that a fortnight before I had had tea with two ladies in the house from which they had vanished two years earlier—while at the same time it was occupied by others! Further, that I had been strongly attracted to a girl who might be a ghost or a dream.

Of course she was neither! But on the other hand what had become of her and her mother? I could not possibly have 'dreamed' of real people of whom I had never heard.

And never since have I heard of them nor met any who knew them. I could, of course, have written to the Harley Street doctor, but such a letter would be difficult enough for me even today. It was beyond the troubled lad of eighteen who was afraid of being taken for a liar or of plunging into troubled waters where he had no business.

So I never solved the mystery and now—but for some very strange chance indeed—I know that I never shall.

The Recurring Tragedy

Post-war business brought William E. Fitchett to England, and pleasure lured him from the great northern manufacturing city down to Arborhaven, there to renew a friendship which had been broken off at the end of his last term at Yale.

Standring was a specialist in nerves and mental diseases. Before the war he had achieved a reputation. During the war his successful treatment of cases roughly diagnosed as shell-shock had brought him world-wide fame. He was still a youngish man, round-faced and kindly-looking, with big searching grey eyes and full head of dark hair flecked here and there with white.

To Fitchett the Tudor mansion, designed in the shape of an E by an architect anxious to do honour to the Virgin Queen, was a place made out of dreams. The first sight one has of it, the gabled pile of mellowed red bricks, standing at the top of long terraces across the water meadows, is something not to be forgotten. The interior is a wonder of crooked floors, oak panelling and beams, great stately rooms, rooms absurdly small, with mysterious little passages and staircases leading to unexpected parts of the house. Here it would seem that time had stood still, had not the men and women who trod the hollow floors changed the fashion of their clothes and the manner of their speech through the three centuries.

'They built real houses in those days,' Fitchett said. 'I don't remember your telling me in the old days that you had a family mansion.'

They were sitting alone in the long dining-room after dinner. The table was an island of light set in a sea of shadows. The gleaming white cloth, the shirt-fronts of the two men, the flowers and silver, the red wine in the glasses, all stood out in shining contrast to the darkness around them. Only an occasional reflection from the fire went questing into the mysterious dimness, and little focuses of light gleamed on the polished surface of furniture or panels.

'I hadn't,' Standring answered. I bought this place only six months ago. It used to belong to General Sir Thomas Shiel.'

'General Shiel.' Fitchett repeated the name as if he were trying to wake a memory. 'Now what did I hear about him? He's dead, isn't he?'

'Yes. Before he died he was one of my patients. I came down here to attend to him. I knew him slightly before. While I was here I fell in love with the house. After his death it came onto the market and I bought it.'

'Yes, yes.' Fitchett's brows were gathered up into a frown. 'But what did I hear about General Shiel? I know there was something.'

'He commanded one of our divisions over in France.'

'Yes, that's right. And didn't he get sent back for making a mess of things—losing a lot of men or something? Wasn't that it?'

'There were questions asked about him in Parliament, certainly.'

'Ah, I thought so.'

'Actually, though, he was invalided home with shell-shock.'

Fitchett laughed and turned a quizzical eye upon his friend.

'Well, that's just your British way of doing things,' he said. 'No general was ever sent back for being incompetent. He was always sick. It sounds so much better.'

The specialist smiled and sipped his wine.

'I can tell you,' he said, 'that the General was in a pretty bad way.'

'Oh, yes; I forgot. He died. And you couldn't cure him. So you're not infallible after all, Standring?'

'I haven't pretended to be. And, mind you, there were several forms of what was popularly known as shell-shock. There was the kind experienced by the poor devil who was blown up, or lay for hours under the wreck of a dug-out. There was another kind which was a polite name for funk. There was also, as you have remarked, the kind which afflicted generals who never went near the line, but about whom questions were asked in the House of Commons.'

'And he had that kind and yet—he died. You should have found him all the easier to cure, Standring.'

'You don't understand. Suppose you came to me and told me you suffered from delusions, and suppose when I inquired their nature you told me that all the grass you saw looked green—what then? Your delusion would consist of your thinking that it ought to be some other colour, and you would be much more difficult to cure. Even if I succeeded in making you think that grass looked red you would be very far from cured.'

Fitchett smiled and broke the long ash from his cigar into a little silver tray at his elbow.

'I see. And if a man tells you he's been seeing ghosts you can only cure him if he's been seeing imaginary ghosts—not real ones. Was that the General's trouble? Did he see ghosts?'

'He did not. At least he didn't say so. But in a sense I suppose he was a haunted man.'

He came to an abrupt pause. Fitchett regarded him with eyebrows slightly raised.

'Well?' he asked. 'I'm not going to pretend that I'm not curious.'

Standring lowered his gaze.

'I'm sorry,' he said, i can't tell you. There's such a thing as professional - '

'Professional secrecy. Professional humbug! Do you remember when we were at Yale, and bitten with the literary bug? I remember one evening we were talking about novels and short stories and the old gag about truth being stranger than fiction. We both agreed that every man, no matter how humdrum his life, had at least one experience which, if he cared to tell it, would make a tremendous story. You may also remember that we agreed to tell each other when the great story in real life came to each of us. Mine hasn't come yet. I rather think yours has.'

'Perhaps it has,' Standring agreed, 'I'm sorry, though, but I can't tell it to you.'

'All right.' Fitchett was plainly disappointed, if you can't, you can't. But listen. Years ago when we made that compact you knew me for a man who could keep his head shut. That was before you joined a profession which made you pigeon-hole your memories and label half of them "secret". I heard some sort of queer story about General Shiel in New York. Who brought it over I can't say. You tell me the truth, and I'll pass it along if that is your wish. If it isn't—next week I leave Liverpool for New York, and I won't say a single word in this country or mine.'

For a little while Standring seemed to consider.

'You can say,' he replied at last, 'that whatever were General Sir Thomas Shiel's faults he suffered for them.'

Fitchett inclined his head.

'I'll say that. And what are you going to tell me? '

'The whole thing if you're really so anxious to hear it and willing to swear to say not a word about it. The General is dead now, and his story—I don't know if that deserves quite to die. At least it's a queer story and there's certainly a moral in it.'

He sat silent a moment, the fingers of one hand on the stem of his half-empty glass, which he rocked slowly to and fro.

'I'd known the General slightly for some time. I knew him when he was a lieutenant-colonel in command of the first battalion of one of the county regiments. He had then the reputation of a martinet, nobody liking him except perhaps one or two of the senior officers. He gained promotion before the war and went out as a brigadier. Afterwards he was given the command of a division. I believe he was pretty thoroughly hated by the men. Every petty annoyance which he could devise to make their lives more miserable he inflicted at a time when life for them was little better than hell. His men all died with their buttons in a high state of polish, their equipment and shrapnel helmets shining. If it sounds splendid it seems at least purposeless. Too much of that sort of thing only harassed them, made them irritable and injured their morale. His orders about prisoners, care of wounded and so on were monumentally brutal. He was a specimen of our own home-grown kind of Prussian, of which there were, fortunately, few. On courts-martial he was extraordinarily severe. He thought only of himself and his own glory. Were it not for another picture which I shall always carry in my mind, I should think of him as a serio-comic goose-stepping figure, with a big sword and a mouthful of oaths. Well, as you know, he ended by losing nine-tenths of the personnel of his division and being sent home'

'With shell-shock,' Fitchett interpolated dryly.

'At least he came home a broken man. Lady Shiel came to see me after a time. She could not get him to put himself into professional hands. She did not tell me much. How much she actually knew I can't say. We made an arrangement. I was to come down to Arborhaven apparently as a guest, actually as a physician. I was to try to win the General's confidence and do what I could for him. In the end I agreed, mostly for the sake of acquaintance, which she was pleased to call friendship.

'I arrived here on a Friday, and Lady Shiel met me at the door. She took me into her husband's study—that small room across the hall—but he was not there at the time, and she went to look for him. While I was there alone I picked up an open book which evidently the General had been reading. The books a patient reads often afford a guide, or at least a finger-post, to his mental state. The book was Eugene Sue's The Wandering Jew.

'When Lady Shiel returned with the General his appearance had a great and very disagreeable effect on me. I will not say that I was shocked, for that is no word for a doctor to use, and yet I do not know of any other word capable of conveying what I mean. To begin with he had aged terribly. From a red-blooded, middle-aged man typical of the Army he had grown old and haggard. Somehow he seemed to have shrunk inside his great frame, like a punctured football. His voice, when he greeted me, had lost its depth of tone. It was as if old age had come upon him in a night.

'Strangest of all he did not impress me as a sick man. His eyes certainly told their tale of suffering, but it was not physical nor yet of that mental kind which any physician may heal. Mind you, in describing this to one of my own profession I should have to consider my words and pick them carefully. To you I tell frankly exactly how I felt about him without stopping to consider any niceties of phraseology. Tell me, have you ever seen a man suffering terribly from remorse, from consciousness of sin? I don't use the phrase in a necessarily pietistic sense.'

Fitchett inclined his head. It was the first movement he had made for some minutes. 'I once saw a man who had been acquitted of murder,' he said. 'Nobody had much doubt about it, although the jury wouldn't convict. I know what you mean.'

'I think you've only a dim idea for all that. It was as if the General bore upon his soul ten thousand crimes, each one ten thousand times worse than murder. I never had much faith in God or devil, heaven or hell until that moment, when I knew that I looked into the eyes of a damned soul. I tell you, Fitchett, my own nerves are pretty sound, and I am not a man whom most would describe as "sensitive", but something like nausea overtook me as I made some kind of pretence to shake his hand.

'I will pass over the early part of the evening and the dreary dinner which followed in this room. There were no other guests, and the Shiels were a childless couple. I found myself dreading the departure of Lady Shiel to the drawing-room. I was almost childishly averse to being left alone with her husband.

'When she had gone, however, I resigned myself to the inevitable, and, at the General's invitation, mixed myself a stiff whisky and soda. I sat where you are sitting now. The General sat here in my place at the head of the table. The low shade of a lamp cut off the light from the upper part of his face, and, thank Heaven, I could scarcely see those dreadful eyes of his.

'He came very abruptly to the point before Lady Shiel had been absent a full minute. "I know exactly why my wife has asked you here," he said, with a kind of weary indifference. "If you cannot see it for yourself I suppose it is hopeless for me to tell you that I am no material for your skill. You will, of course, persist in trying to cure me?"

' "As you have guessed, that is why I am here," I answered.

'He poured himself out a stiff tot of whisky, and regarded me with a mirthless smile.

' "Of course," he said, "this is the first thing I am to give up?"

'"That and morbid books," I answered.

'"Oh, you mean The Wandering Jew? Do you know the story?"

" 'I haven't read Eugene Sue's book, but I know the legend. He passes from life to life, doesn't he? And cannot die until Christ's second coming? I have heard various accounts of the legend. Christ on His way to Calvary had fallen under the weight of His Cross. One of the crowd struck Him and urged Him to go faster. Christ replied: 'I go on, but you shall linger until I return.'

' "Some accounts have it that the Wandering Jew was Pilate's porter, others that he was one of the Pharisees, a shoemaker."

' "He was neither," said the General, as if he were stating an item of authentic news. "He was Judas Iscariot."

' "That is quite new to me," I said.

'"He was Judas Iscariot," he repeated. "He stood jeering with the crowd, and Christ fell at his feet—the Cross was so heavy—and Judas—Judas was so eager to show that he had renounced his Master. He kicked Him as He lay fainting and said: 'What are you feigning, Man?' And Christ, presently rising up, gazed at him and—and spoke that dreadful sentence."
'The General's voice shook terribly, and the words ended in a whisper.

'"Who told you that version?" I asked as lightly as I could.

'"Who told me?" he repeated. "Who told me?" He let his face fall between his hands and groaned aloud. "Oh, my God, if somebody had only told me!" He raised his face once more. "Do you know why Judas betrayed his Master? I can tell you that, too. It was pride. His some-time friends had jeered at him for a follower of the charlatan who pretended to be the Messiah, the King of the Jews. It wasn't for the thirty silver coins—it was all pride!"

'He spoke with an uncanny air of certainty and ended with a deep shuddering groan. Rather belatedly, perhaps, I thought it best to change the topic of conversation.'

' "Come General," I said. "I don't think too much theorising about Scriptural matters is good for you. I am here to try to do something for you. If you don't mind my asking a few questions so soon after dinner –"

'He cut me short with a motion of his hand.

' "My dear doctor," he said, "I will tell you the whole truth about myself, as far as I know it. If, after having heard what I am going to tell you, you still think that my malady comes within the scope of science, then—I was going to say for the sake of peace—I will submit myself to your hands. You will probably regard me as an interesting case, but you will not have much time in which to experiment upon me. First, I know, you require perfect frankness. You shall have it. And I had better begin by stating that just as a few rare men have never been able to understand the meaning of the word fear, so I have never understood the meaning of the word sympathy. I know it to be a sensation which makes people shrink from hurting others, but I never experienced it.

' "I have had the reputation of a hard, proud, ambitious man. I have earned it. The men under my command hated and feared me, not without cause. I wanted them to. I had my head full of the hard great men of old times: Moor, who lashed men for breaking step on the march; the swearing, steel-hearted Iron Duke. I wanted my name to go down to history coupled with names like these. My great aim was to win battles, to take ground, not for the sake of my country, but for the reputation of General Sir Thomas Shiel."

' "He had no heart, no feeling. He was an automaton, but what an automaton! What a soldier! Almost I could see the printed word.

' "To that end my men had to be the smartest in France. I caused them to be continually harried while they were resting. While they were in the line my brigade staffs continually went round to see that their buttons, boots, and equipment were as brilliantly polished as if they were parading on the barrack square. It mattered nothing to me what rest and sleep I deprived them of. Those last letters home, which might have been written and were not, troubled me not at all. I was the Iron General; they were my soldiers, my pawns. When men were sniped at night because of the moonlight shining on a polished shrapnel helmet it mattered nothing to me. Men were cheap enough. England was full of them; the bases were full of them; long processions of drafts thronged all the lines of communication. One asked for men and got them, as if one were indenting for quantities of soap or rifle oil. I did not mind sacrificing lives to enhance my reputation. I wanted to command an army; I might even rise to be Commander-in-Chief if the war lasted long enough. There was no end to my ambition.

' "I had orders at last to move my division on to the Somme, to take part in one of those attacks which proved so disastrous. My division had a certain objective. I gave my brigades orders that they had to take it. There must be no flinching or bungling. I warned them. If a unit failed to take its objective, whatever the cause, it must attack and attack again so long as there was one man left. I said it, I meant it, and I stuck to it. I was the Iron General until the end.

' "I had my headquarters in a little village called Flarincourt. There was a small white chateau a few hundred yards to the north where my staff and myself were housed. We arrived some days before the troops, and as the trains at the railhead disgorged them I myself took the 'march past", sitting my horse at the roadside, my hand at the salute, while the doomed battalions tramped past me in columns of fours. There were motor-omnibuses waiting from them at the next village, and the men hated them as forerunners of disaster.

' "I had watched the last battalion of a brigade march past, and, knowing no other troops were due to arrive for some hours, rode off with an officer on my staff for lunch at the chateau. Opposite the chateau gates was a roadside Calvary, the Cross raised high and almost surrounded by poplars, but with an opening of the trees in front, made—so it seemed to me later—so that Christ might look down and marvel at the ways of men two thousand years after His own passion and death. Close against the Calvary, and in the shade of the poplars, a private soldier sprawled on the grass in an attitude of acute exhaustion. His face was pale and damp with sweat. To the sleeves of his tunic, below the numerals on his shoulder-straps, was sewn the divisional sign which marked him as one of my men and a straggler from one of the battalions which had just marched down the road.

' "Just then we were getting men from employment at the bases and from the non-combatant forces, men who had hitherto been declared unfit for service in the front line.

They were hastily passed as 'fit' by medical boards and drafted into fighting units after a few days' training. Some of them were fit for the work and others were not. I had a reputation to retain with men who came under my notice for falling out on the march. I reined up at once.

'Hi, you, man,' I shouted, 'what are you doing there?'

' "He neither stirred nor answered, and in a trice I was off my horse and standing beside him, shouting and cursing. The man was clean-shaven, and his short hair was auburn-brown. I started a little when I saw his face, for I fancied I had seen him somewhere before. I knew the wide brow and the pair of large, deep, sorrowful brown eyes which he opened to look up into my face. The lower part of his face I did not recognise, but that brow and those eyes were strangely, insistently familiar. There was something else which affected me queerly. I put it down to some optical illusion, due to the sun's rays and the shrapnel helmet. When I first looked at him it seemed as if blood were trickling down his forehead. Then, as I looked closer, it was gone.

' "Why can't you stand up," I bawled, "when an officer speaks to you? What are you feigning, man?"

' "I must have fainted,' he answered in a gentle cultured voice. One hand strayed round to his shoulders and touched the great square pack which was strapped upon them. 'It is so heavy,' he said.

' "I cursed and kicked him, told him to get up at once and go on, and stood over him while he struggled to his feet. I did not care if he were shamming or not. If he were, he would go on his way with a wholesome lesson. If he were not, he might drop down again and die for all I cared. He was no use to the Army in that event, and I cared nothing of what happened to men who could not march and shoot.

' "With great difficulty and much obvious suffering he rose to his feet. Then he stood still for a moment and looked at me. 'This has happened before,' he said very slowly and distinctly, and added: 'You will remember.'

' "Something—I do not know what—prevented me from questioning him as to his words. It seemed absurd at the time, but an unaccountable sensation of fear stole over me. The curse died on my lips as the man turned his back on me and began slowly and painfully to limp down the road. I remounted my horse and rode up to the chateau for lunch—wondering.

' "Next day occurred an incident which I forgot immediately afterwards for the time being. A party of men with a sergeant in charge was passing the chateau, proceeding on some duty or other. I came out immediately behind them so that, although they did not see me, I could hear them talking. 'Your pack 'urts you, does it?' shouted the sergeant to one of them. 'Well, you look up there.' He nodded towards the Calvary. 'Jesus Christ 'ad to carry something a blank sight 'eavier!' I do not know if he meant to be profane or if it were merely his rough way of offering consolation. But I remembered the incident later.

' "From the next day I was busy. Before dawn the muttering, rumbling, and fluttering of gunfire began. It continued all day and the next night, increasing to drum-fire before the following dawn. Shortly afterwards the first reports came in. The day had gone ill with us. Our attack had broken down. I sent out the order: 'Attack again immediately. Every objective must be taken.' It was the sort of order that any of the great generals might have issued. It made me one with them—I, the Iron General.

' "All that day and the next panic reports came in from all the brigade headquarters. The enemy along our front was impregnably placed so long as he held out on the left and right. I knew it was so. I think a kind of madness seized me. To send the remnants of those battalions again and again to the attack was like flinging spray against a rock. But my pride weighed down all discretion. I was the Iron General who had never drawn back from what he set out to do. I cared for nothing but that reputation. From the safe distance of my chateau, far from the welter of mud and blood, I sent out the order repeatedly: 'Attack again! Attack again!' And my big battalions melted and melted and melted, and long processions of Red Cross vans thundered past the chateau, and still I sent to my rebellious brigadiers the same mad command: 'Attack again!'

'"You know' how it ended, the thousands I sacrificed on the altar of my pride. That's ancient history now. When the final crash came, in the shape of a peremptory order from the Army Command, I was like a man dazed. Then, through my bewilderment streamed the light of old and dreadful memories. He had told me I should remember. I did remember! I did remember!"

'The General's voice rose to a scream. His face worked horribly and he clenched his hands and beat them upon the table, close by where I am sitting now, in a kind of frenzy.

'"What did you remember?" I asked him.

'"It was the soldier's face first of all—the soldier who had fainted under the weight of his pack beside the Calvary. I thought I knew it. I did know it. Everybody knows it. O God, have mercy—mercy!"

'I drew a long breath and sat still and staring. "Ye did it unto Me". The words shaped themselves in my brain and kept repeating themselves. The General's voice broke out again:

'"Don't you see? Don't you understand?" he snivelled. "It was He I cursed and kicked as He lay fainting by the roadside, just as I had cursed and kicked Him on His way to that other death two thousand years ago. Oh, yes, I remembered that, too! It all came back so clearly across the centuries, even to the memory of how the blood-money in my pouch had jingled as I asked Him what He was feigning. I remembered all—all. How they laughed at me for a follower of Him . . . the leering High Priest of the Temple with his bag of money ... the kiss in the Garden. And I remembered passages out of other lives since then, for death with me is scarcely a breathing space between one life and another. And in each of these lives I have betrayed my fellow-man because of the pride that is my heritage and curse through all the ages. I can look back until my mind reels upon betrayal after betrayal in my many lives, down to the day when, because of my pride, I betrayed those thousands in that hell upon the Somme. For that is my punishment!—to go on living and betraying, to live in many lands and under many names, but always to be Judas."

'He fell forward and began to weep unpleasantly, great rending sobs that seemed to tear his throat. "If I'd only known Him," he whimpered, "when He lay by the roadside outside Flarincourt, He might have forgiven me at last! I might have saved myself! But I must go on ... I must go on to the same End which only marks another Beginning."'

Standring brought his story to an abrupt conclusion. His cigar had gone out, and he sought for and lit another. Fitchett waited a little while, as if he expected more to come.

'Is that all?' he said at last.

'That is all the General's story, as he told it to me.'

'But what about the end?'

'The end? Oh, you know that. I treated the General, and failed. You knew that from the beginning. I think you remarked that I wasn't infallible.'

'But what did the General die of? One doesn't generally die of a hallucination, does one?'

'No. My dear fellow, surely you can guess. You remember what happened to Judas Iscariot, don't you?'

'Not'

'Yes. The General hanged himself from that long beam out there in the hall.'

Father of the Man

Without stopping to wonder how he came to be there at all, Raymond Tallifer passed under a familiar archway and walked through a short stone passage into a long, cool corridor.

The place was as silent as an empty church; it held, in fact, an atmosphere like that of a deserted place of worship. It was paved with large square stones which rang underfoot and awoke echoes overhead, and which had been worn and hallowed by many generations of schoolboys. One side was lined by windows looking out upon the quadrangle, and for each window there was a little blaze in which the motes were playing and a distorted rectangle of light upon the far wall. This was hung with severe engravings depicting such subjects as the Forum at Rome, the ruins of Carthage, the circus at Pompeii. In the middle there was a board covered with red baize, to which many typed notices were pinned.

It was more than twenty years since Tallifer had stood in that corridor, and he was aware now of having happened upon a place which was barred and sealed against the access of time. He might have seen it an hour since for all the change apparent to him. An hour or a quarter of a century; it was all the same. The corridor had its own degree of coolness and its own subtle unseizable odour. This was neither quite the harsh smell of aggressive cleanliness associated with hospitals, nor the odour of an old building in the process of decaying, but a subtle blend of both combined with something unique and characteristic. Whatever changes had taken place in a mutable world during the past twenty-and-something years, the 'college stink' remained the same.

Tallifer was moved after a fashion which he would have been incapable of describing. His heartstrings became vocal, and quivered and wailed to an old, lost tune. He had not seen his old school since that last morning when he stood up in chapel to sing, 'Lord, dismiss us with Thy blessing', with all the roads of the world lying open before him. However remiss they may be in their attentions to the dear old lady, there are few men who have not a deep and abiding love for their Alma Mater, and it is a pleasant emotional experience to return at long last and see the calm old face unchanged by any added line or wrinkle. Tallifer was an old Schoolhouse boy. It pleased him to think that, whatever changes might have overtaken the other houses—and he knew of two new ones since his day—Schoolhouse seemed as immutable as the pyramids.

It was a Saturday afternoon, enough in itself to account for the interior being deserted. From outside there came faint and far sounds, as sweet to Tallifer as the humming of bees— boys' voices and the hard, crisp impact of leather against bats. Tallifer walked to the west end of the corridor and thoughtfully climbed some stone steps. He supposed he should have called on the headmaster, but it amused him to walk about as if he were a boy once more. Sooner or later, he supposed, he would meet somebody, and then he would be able to explain.

Outside a door he paused with his hand on the latch. In his day this had given entrance to the House library, and he supposed it still did. He waited a moment before entering, trying to conjure a picture of the room as he had seen it last. It was here that he had first discovered for himself the delights of Sterne and the purple passages in Byron.

The latch clicked under his hand and the heavy door swung open before him. There were the same tables and cane-backed chairs and the same litter of magazines and newspapers. It seemed to him that even the same books stood on the cedar shelves, for here and there familiar bindings caught his gaze. Even the one occupant of the room, a boy who sat reading with his elbows on a table, and his head resting in his hands, looked strangely and even breath-takingly familiar to the visitor.

The boy looked up, and then rose with the easy smartness of a soldier coming to attention, and stood waiting with a shy boyish smile. He was about fourteen, and wore the regulation uniform of the lower school, a black coat, dark grey trousers, and Eton collar. The fact of the collar being worn outside proclaimed him to be in his first year.

'Sit down,' said Tallifer, wondering where he could have seen the youngster before, 'and don't mind me. I'm only an Old Boy come back to have a look round. Why aren't you at cricket?'

He put the question casually in a tone of civil inquiry, and the boy replied readily and smilingly.

'I crocked my knee, sir, so I got leave to fag. Of course, I could go out and watch, but the Firsts are playing away and the Seconds have only got a rotten match, so I thought I'd stay in and read. A chap at school doesn't get many chances of being alone, except some of the big fellows who have studies to themselves.'

Tallifer smiled.

'You like being alone, then?' he asked.

'Oh, no, not much, sir, but just now and then. A chap sometimes wants a chance to be quiet and think.'

'Ah,' said Tallifer, 'I remember feeling like that, too. It's an odd thing, but I remember doing exactly as you're doing when I was about your age. I'd crocked my knee and spent the afternoon here and—what's that book you're reading?'

'Tom Brown's Schooldays,' answered the boy, and held it up for him to see.

Tallifer exclaimed aloud.

'Well,' he added, 'this is too remarkable! I remember that I started reading Tom Brown's Schooldays on that occasion, and I fell asleep over it and had a horrible dream which I couldn't remember when I woke up.'

The boy smiled broadly.

'Perhaps it bored you, sir. I don't think I like it very much. It may have been good when it was written, but it isn't a bit like school life today. But Mr Frankham, our English master, told us that everybody ought to read it, so I've begun.'

'Old Frankham still here, then?' thought Tallifer, smiling. 'I must go and look him up ... Do you like being at school?' he asked aloud.

'Yes, I think so, sir,' the boy answered doubtfully, 'but it's different from what I expected it to be. Of course, I'd read the usual sort of stories in which the hero's a real wonder, and the butler's an ex-convict in league with one of the masters who is a crook, and the boys have the most wonderful rags which couldn't happen at any real school. We have rags, of course, and they're very funny ones, but they wouldn't seem a bit funny if we told anybody else about them, and nobody would think it worth while putting them in a book. And there's nobody here in the least like a hero, except Graceman'

'Graceman!'

'Do you know him, sir? He's captain of the eleven; but there's never anything heroic for him to do, except knock up centuries sometimes.'

Tallifer stood staring hard and straight at the boy, gripping the edges of the table. And suddenly the boy coloured and looked abashed. 'I haven't been talking too much, have I?' he asked awkwardly.

'No, no! Go on, go on!'

'I feel that I could tell you things, things that I couldn't tell anybody else, not to my father or my mother or my best friend. I wonder why I can tell them to you.'

'Ah!' said Tallifer gently and very sadly. 'I think I know.'

'It's funny how we can't tell other people all about ourselves. I get thousands of thoughts and ambitions which aren't anything to be ashamed of, and yet I think I should die if anybody knew them—anybody but you. It's funny how little my father and mother really know about me, and I expect I know just as little about them. I couldn't bear that anybody should know how fond I am of Dick Saltash—except perhaps Dick himself, and then I couldn't stand it if he mentioned it. I don't know why, except that it would seem so sloppy and girlish.

'Dick's my friend. When I first met him here I thought we were going to live in a sort of school story, and that one of us was going to be the hero and the other the sort of second hero. I think I'd kill myself if any of the fellows knew that. But it wasn't like what we thought it was going to be, and neither of us is anything like a hero. Dick isn't because he funks Bums minor and gets out of fighting him. And I funk Bums minor too. I can't see the sense of fighting when you know you'll get beaten.

'In all the school stories the two boys who have had a fight shake hands and become friends for life, and it's always the bully who gets beaten. Even if I beat him I couldn't be friends with him, because he bounds horribly and I should think his people are cads. He doesn't bully like they do in the school stories, but he bags your books and breaks your pens and says rotten things, and when you get first to a fives court he comes and roots you out and swears blind he's bagged it first.

'Boys don't talk as they're made to talk in books. They've got much more sense than grown-up people think, they know more about things, and they're not so—healthy, I suppose is the word. They're very snobbish, too. There are thousands of things you must do, or you mustn't, for no reason at all, and there's the right and the wrong sorts of slang. School life isn't a bit like what I thought it was going to be like.'

'Nothing ever is,' said Tallifer, with a slow, sad smile; 'but I know how useless it is to tell you that. We paint our own pictures of the future, and then we have to scrape them out and paint others. But we continue so until the end, feeding on hope. What do you think you're going to do with your life, my boy?'

He looked up brightly.

'I know what I want to do,' he said, i couldn't tell anybody else, but I can tell you.'

Just for a moment Tallifer winced and leaned heavily on the table.

'No, don't tell me,' he said, with a catch in his voice, 'it isn't fair!' His face worked for a moment. 'Go on,' he said presently, i know that I am not a free agent. I know that I must listen.'

The boy uttered a high, clear laugh.

'I don't know what that means,' he said. 'Am I a free agent?'

'I have already told you that I am not, and you - But you don't yet understand. Come, tell me! I know already what you are going to say, and I suppose I deserve to hear it.'

'Well,' began the boy, i want to be like Graceman when I'm his age, and afterwards I want to be a county cricketer and play for Surrey. Graceman will very likely be asked to play for Surrey during the holidays. He is going on to Oxford, and is almost certain of his Blue. So I should like to play for Surrey, too, when I'm old enough, and after that I want to be a soldier and win the V.C.

'I should be horribly ragged if the other fellows knew just that, and even Dick would rag me. But I can tell you. My father says he can't afford to send me into the Army, but he says there's almost certain to be war with Germany before many years, so then everybody will have to fight, and I may get a show. Oh, and I want to have a wonderful collection of stamps. Perhaps one day I'll buy a collection at a sale among a lot of old books, and there'll be a twopenny blue Mauritius in it, and Sydney views, and lots of triangular Capes.

'And afterwards I suppose I shall want to marry. I don't think much of girls, but fellows seem to when they get older, so I expect I'll be like all the rest. It wouldn't be so bad if I could find one who wasn't stupid, and had been brought up like a boy, and wouldn't mind racing me downhill on a bike and going to watch cricket and footer matches. And I want to live in an old house in the country, with panelled walls and a ghost, and find an old treasure in a secret hiding-place. And, of course, I want to have tons and tons of money, so that I can have a good time myself and be kind to the poor. And, of course, I want old Dick to live near me, and have a nice wife like mine. And I want to do heaps and heaps of noble and generous things without anybody ever thinking that I was pi. And I don't want ever to get old and die; and perhaps by the time I'm about forty they'll have invented something that'll let people go on living for as long as they like. And whatever happens, I want people to say of me, "Well, he was a good sportsman and he always played the game."'

Tallifer turned away, and for a moment his eyes were dim.

'Old chap,' he then said, 'it won't be a bit like that.'

The boy's face fell, but it lit up again after a moment,

'It might be,' he said. 'Nobody knows.'

Tallifer regarded him pitifully.

'I know,' he said, 'and not merely because I am forty and speaking to fourteen. You have learned already that nothing is as you expected it to be and hoped it would be, but you will go on cheating yourself until death steals your last breath out of your body. And your ambitions which would make most men laugh, and make me weep, you will shed as now you discard your outgrown clothes. And those with which you will replace them will be more reasonable and less worthy, but even these you will never attain, nor those which will follow and follow until the end.

'You will come to laugh at your dreams of playing county cricket, and give up the game when you find that you are, after all, only one of many thousands of muddlers. You will have your taste of war and endure the agony of having your courage tried and found wanting at your own tribunal. You will see in it nothing gallant nor soul-stirring, but a heart-sickening companionship with mud, vermin, and misery, long months of foulness and boredom punctuated by moments of indescribable terror. And you will win no V.C., but some small, tawdry decoration they will give you for having done, perhaps, a tithe of your duty.'

'How can you know all this?' the boy interrupted, hardly above a whisper.

'Let me go on. And your tomboy sweetheart you will neither seek nor find, but you will kill the love of a good woman and go searching greedily for shams and base imitations, which are all that the world will have to offer you. Your idols will fall from their clay pedestals, and you will not pick them up nor have the courage to set others in their place, but sneer at yourself, because once you were their worshipper. What you call friendship now will some day come to be a myth to you; you will count as your friends those whose society is just endurable to you.

'You will never have your fine country home, nor will you be so simple and wholesome as to go and breathe God's pure air through a cottage window. You will live in the crowded places where men go to poison their souls and bodies. You will lose that clean taste in your mouth. You will feel the shackles upon you and have no will to break them, and drink to forget what you have become. You will play with unclean and unwholesome toys, and lose all taste for the sweeter things of life. And when you are scarcely past your youth you will come to the last hope of all—that God Who knows all and understands all human weaknesses may perhaps pardon all.' And the boy looked at him piteously and raised a cry.

'It isn't true!' he cried, it can't be true! I am beginning to hate you, although I can tell you everything that is in my heart.'

'It is natural that you should hate me,' Tallifer answered, 'and it is true. Indeed, it has already happened, for time is not merely something that creeps around the edge of a clock; it is a plastic substance in the hands of the Almighty.'

The boy dropped his head between his hands.

'Who are you?' he asked.

'I will even tell you that,' said Tallifer, his voice vibrant with pity, 'for you will wake in a moment and mercifully forget. Yes, you will go on feeding on hope, and only remember that you had a bad dream which your first moment of waking sponged from your mind. And I must pity you, and you must hate me, and there is nothing in you heart which you cannot tell me, because I am you and you are me; because you are the boy I once was, and I am the man you will become.'

At that the boy screamed and recoiled, and his face was a mask of terror and loathing. But Tallifer stretched out his hands towards his lost youth, and in his heart there was a great tenderness, stronger than mother-love. 'No, no, don't hate me! Pity—pity'

Another voice chimed in upon his own; a voice coming out of another world. And the boy slowly faded with the room, and the bookcase and the tables, and the last that Tallifer saw of him was the horror in his eyes.

The woman who was not Tallifer's wife had come into the room and awakened him. She was dressed to go out. In fact, she was on the stage, and due to set out for the evening performance. She was a hipless person, with a vapid and much-painted countenance. Tallifer blinked at her, at the familiar furniture of the flat dining-room, and at the coloured bottles and cocktail shaker which stood ready to hand on the bare, polished table.

'I wish you wouldn't mutter so much in your sleep,' she said, 'if I were you. I'd cut down the drinks a bit during the day. I'm just off. You might let me have my taxi fare. I haven't any change.'

He felt in his pocket for small silver and handed it to her. She turned towards the door.

'Don't forget,' she said, 'that you're meeting me after the show, and taking me to supper at the Eighty-Eight!'

'All right, Billie,' Tallifer muttered. 'Goodbye!'

He watched her go. Then he let his face sink between his hands, and groaned.

Fellow Travellers

I broke my journey at Bandingdon, and with a reason. It was a piece of pure sentiment which caused me to make Bandingdon the end of my stage, and sent me to The Black Bear, the ancient barracks of an inn which faced the Town Hall across the empty cattle-pens in the market square.

The little town on the Great North Road has shrunken and grown sleepier since the days when the coaches passed through it on their way to and from York. The Black Bear has now little use for its fifty bedrooms. The great coffee-room, where hungry travellers once made hasty meals and listened to the crack of whips and the trampling of hoofs in the yard outside, is now used only when the gayer spirits of Bandingdon conspire to dance. The great stables in the yard are nearly empty, save on market days, and instead of a farrier you will find a mechanic, who lives under a board labelled 'Garage'.

I pushed my motor bicycle into the yard, and rang the ostler's bell. It was a find old bell-pull, heavy and rusty, and might well have been the same that my grandfather had seized on a certain June night before Victoria was queen.

A youth came and took the motor bicycle from me, and I entered the house through a low door in the side of the archway.

The bar was typical of that sort of house, spacious, solidly furnished, and decorated with sporting prints and one or two stuffed specimen fish. I found my way to the office, booked one of the fifty bedrooms, and returned to the bar, where an austere, middle-aged woman sat enshrined behind a window. There was nobody to talk to. The only other occupants of the room were a man who had been fishing and looked tired out, and a farmer whose face belied him if he were not morose.

An oppressive air of sadness brooded over the place, as if the old hostel were a conscious and living thing, and had passed into a sad old age reflecting on it former glories in the days of horses. Perhaps it was because I knew a sad story connected with the house and with my family. I only know that I felt a most unwonted depression as I sat in a comer washing some of the road dust from my throat with a glass of beer.

A heavy grandfather clock ticked sonorously, and that was the only sound heard in the room for a full five minutes, save once when the morose farmer banged his glass down upon the counter and demanded more whisky of the morose barmaid.

Presently the door opened and an aged waiter came in and looked around.

He approached me, and bending over, asked in a low voice:

'Are you the gentleman who's staying here the night?'

'Yes, I'm staying the night,' I said.

'Then what time would you like your dinner?'

I looked at the grandfather, and saw that it was twenty minutes to eight.

'Oh, any time convenient,' I answered. 'I shall want a wash first and change my collar.'

'Very good, sir. Your knapsack's been taken up to your room. Say, eight o'clock then, sir. I can show you your room now if you wish.'

'All right,' I said, and got up on my legs.

I followed him through the vestibule and up a fine oak staircase on to a broad landing where I drew abreast of him.

'Not many people staying here?' I asked.

'Oh, no, sir. There's only you and a lady, and she wouldn't be here if her car hadn't broken down. You see, sir, we don't cater much for commercials.

They mostly go to The Cross Keys. Not like the old days here, sir.'

He spoke of them as if he remembered them, and set me smiling.

'This is your room, sir. Number four. You'll ring if you want anything. Will you go straight to the coffee-room if you're ready, or shall I find you in the bar?'

'I expect,' I said, 'you'll find me in the bar. I don't know where the coffee-room is.'

'Very good, sir, I'll find you there.' He gave me an ingenuous smile.

'You didn't mind me suggesting you should dine at eight, sir? You see, the young lady has given her order to dine then, and if you have yours along with her it'll save some trouble downstairs.'

'Oh, that's all right,' I said, moving further into my bedroom. I was not, at the time, at all interested in the young, lady.

Bandingdon is a great deal less than half-way to Harrogate, whither I was on my way to stay with friends. I had a long ride before me on the following day, and I began to regret the impulse which had brought me to stay a night in the town and at this gloomy, half-deserted hotel.

But I was committed to it now, and reflecting that it was only for a few hours, I washed, put on a clean collar from my knapsack—most of my luggage having preceded me by train—and went downstairs.

At five minutes past eight the waiter called me from the bar and conducted me into a small room, panelled in dark oak, where the white cloth of a table laid for two gleamed brightly under a chandelier.

I have said that the old coffee-room was now closed, save for occasional dances. In the old days, when the house was busy, the room in which I now found myself doubtless accommodated any overflow or parties desirous of dining alone. I could wager that the great mahogany sideboard had been there for a hundred years; indeed, how human ingenuity had devised a means of getting it into the room was a matter for speculation. The room was not overloaded with furniture, and the management had had the good taste to refrain from plastering the panels with pictures. There was a fine, high fireplace, carved out of the same oak as the walls, solid old mahogany chairs, and a fine old dinner wagon. I don't suppose the room had changed in any essential since the eighteen-thirties, and suddenly I thought:

'This must be the very room! It wouldn't have been the great coffee-room. They'd have asked for a little room—those two on their way to Gretna.'

The waiter held back a chair for me, and I sat down. There was only one long table, and he had laid my place so that I should sit elbow to elbow with my fellow guest. A minute later she entered the room.

She was very young; perhaps twenty-one or twenty-two; and she was tall for a girl, and slim, and very quiet and graceful in her movements. She was fair, with a brown tinge in her hair, a pink transparent complexion, a nose that was slightly aquiline, and melting blue eyes.

The moment she came in I seemed to recognise her. I had risen and my lips had come apart to greet her, and memory was fumbling for her name.

She gave me one calm glance, then went over to the bell and touched it. And as she looked at me I knew that I had made some unaccountable mistake, that she and I were strangers after all.

I felt hot and embarrassed. She had seen that I had been about to speak. And why hadn't I spoken? People forced into the intimacy of taking a meal at the same table may surely pass a casual remark. That mistaken recognition had thrown me for a moment off my balance. And now, as I looked at her profile, I knew that I had never met anyone at all closely resembling her. Why, then, I asked myself, had I made this strange error and so nearly created an embarrassing situation?

In came the waiter with our dinner, a very simple, prosaic meal, with a first course consisting of steak and vegetables. He set the dish and two plates before me, and we took our seats.

The girl rejected the wine list with a motion of her hand.

'I'll have some coffee later on, please,' she said.

I ordered half a bottle of Beaune and our waiter departed in search of it.

I was rather grateful to him for making it necessary to say something to her.

'May I give you some of this?' I asked, 'I see I am expected to do the honours.'

'Please,' she said, raising her eyes. 'No, not quite all that, thank you. That will do beautifully. Thank you very much.'

Quite a good deal can be said in accompaniment to so common an office as passing the salt and mustard. She responded to me quite frankly and naturally, and we were fairly started in casual conversation by the time the waiter reappeared with a small and dusty bottle.

'Are you motoring?' she asked.

'Motor-cycling,' I answered, 'I hope to get to Harrogate tomorrow night.'

'You've a long way before you.'

'I know. I should have gone further today but I wanted to stay the night here. I know you're motoring, too. I've heard about your misfortune.'

She looked up and smiled.

'Oh, have you? Yes, it's an awful nuisance. The clutch slipped and I couldn't get on. I've got to wait until tomorrow to have it re-lined. I'm thirty-five miles from home and there are no more trains to the village station. The people at the garage here wanted four pounds ten to drive me home, and I simply wouldn't pay it. In any event I should have had to come back for the car tomorrow or sent my brother. So I rang them up at home to explain things, and decided to spend the night here.'

'You might have met with worse fortune,' I said. 'This is a charming old inn.'

'Isn't it? But it's so long outlived its prosperous days that one can't help feeling sorry for it.'

I looked at her sharply.

'It's rather strange that you should say that,' I said, 'for it's exactly what I've been thinking. These old walls could tell some strange tales if they could speak. The late Mr Richard Turpin might have come in here for a hasty meal if he really accomplished that mythical ride of his.'

'Yes,' she said, 'we're on the road to York, aren't we?'

'This is more than merely the road to York,' I said, it's the road to Gretna. I wonder how many couples arrived here on their way to the old blacksmith's, and bribed the ostler to look out for a chaise with yellow wheels and an infuriated Papa. I know of at least one.'

She laughed gently.

'Ah,' she said, 'we're not so romantic now. Modem inventions have killed all that. A hundred years ago no news could travel faster than a horse. It's no use for runaway couples to travel at sixty miles an hour, when the telegraph and telephone can beat them, and set the police to work to waylay them—if the lady is under age—before they have fairly started. It was the railways and the telegraph which brought an end to the Gretna marriages.'

'And the law,' I said.

'Yes, and the law too. But mostly railway trains. They had to use the quickest means of transport, poor things, and it can't be half so romantic to elope in a railway train as it would be in a post-chaise.'

'Personally,' I said, 'I haven't tried either.'

The feeble joke set us both laughing, and then a spell of silence fell between us. Strange how we should have chanced upon the topic of the Gretna marriages in The Black Bear at Bandingdon. And yet not so strange, for my subconscious mind must have been full of my grandfather's romance.

My companion was thinking of something. I watched a play of emotions on her face, like light and shade. Was she thinking, I wondered, of all the happy, timorous couples, now long dead, who had passed under the archway of the inn—bonneted maidens of bashful seventeen, whiskered bridegrooms of one-and-twenty? Such pictures one could visualise! Heavy fathers armed with pistols, breathing ripe Georgian oaths; little Misses being taken home in tears; servant maids in mob caps vowing that it was a shame; Edwin, bereft of his bride, drinking brandy at the bar and swearing to end his life.

'You know,' she said, with a sudden smile, 'there ought to be ghosts here.'

'There ought!' I said.

Perhaps there were. Perhaps there was an invisible shadowy company about us—my grandfather at my elbow touching me with a spirit hand and giving me flashes of memory which were none of mine by right.

Who shall say?

'Please smoke,' said the girl. 'I know you want to.'

The waiter had cleared the table of the remains of our meal, but we sat on, talking. A strange intimacy had sprung up between us, as if we had known each other a long while, instead of being strangers who did not even know each other's names.

I offered her my cigarette case, but she declined it. Then I lit a cigarette for myself and leaned back.

'Do you know,' I said, 'I nearly dropped an appalling brick when you came into the room. I thought I knew you. It must have been some trick of the light. I was just going to say, "Hullo, Miss, fancy meeting you here!" and only discovered just in time that I couldn't find a name to fill in the blank. Then, at the same moment I realised that I'd never met anybody even resembling you. I think I should have fled from the room or hidden under the table if I had said it.'

She smiled. It was a rather mystified little smile.

'That's strange,' she said, lingering a moment on the last word. 'I had almost the same experience. Not when I first came into the room, but while you were speaking to the waiter. I thought, "Now' where can I have seen him before?" And the next moment I knew that I had never seen you before. It's rather uncanny, isn't it?'

I agreed that it was. I agreed more emphatically in my own mind than I expressed in words. There was another spell of silence.

'D'you know Bandingdon?' she asked at last. 'I suppose there's nothing thrilling to do here of an evening?'

'I expect,' I said, 'there is only the eternal Pictures.'

She made a little gesture of horror.

'Spare me,' she said, 'the cinematograph in a small country town!'

'I was hoping,' I remarked, 'that you'd go on talking to me.'

'I'm afraid,' she said with a laugh, 'you'll have to do most of the talking. My fund of conversation is very soon exhausted. I wonder if they've got a book here with the history of the inn? There might be some interesting stories.'

'I know,' I said, 'at least one, but I doubt if it's in any book.'

'About the inn?'

'About the inn, and about an elopement, and about my grandfather.'

'How thrilling! Do tell me.'

'If it won't bore you. As a matter of fact, it's on account of the story that I broke my journey here. I shouldn't be surprised if the whole thing had happened in this very room.'

'No! Really!' She was smiling with interest and curiosity. 'How very extraordinary!'

'First of all,' I began, 'my father was getting on towards middle life when I was born, and so was his father when he was born, or, rather, his father must have been well on in the fifties. My grandfather was born in 1803.

'My people were not of much account socially. They were prosperous enough and well-to-do, as yeoman farmers who practised thrift generally were in those days. My grandfather shook hands with the squire, but he knew his place. "God bless the squire and his relations, and keep us in our proper stations"—I daresay he sang that in his youth. It's almost a pity for his sake that he didn't practise the sentiment when he grew up, for in the early 'twenties he fell in love with the squire's daughter, and Miss, possibly because he was verboten, responded to his suit. The result was an elopement, with Gretna as the intended destination.

'But things went wrong for the ill-fated pair. I don't know quite what happened. Probably they didn't get such a long start as they had hoped for. Possibly they were badly served with horseflesh at the stages along the road, and the squire met with better luck. All that family history records is that they broke the journey here for a meal, and bribed the ostler—who was probably used to that sort of work—to keep a sharp lookout for any signs of pursuit, and if possible to put the pursuers off the scent.

'Now the old squire was hot on their heels, and doubtless he knew it because people along the road would have described the runaway pair to him. At least he would have none of the ostler's bluff, and came stamping into the room where they sat at table—perhaps this very room—and put an abrupt period on the romance. He had the law on his side, you see. If my grandfather had resisted him there would have been a duel, and the poor little lady would have lost either her father or her lover.

'But I like the way my grandfather behaved. He might not have been good enough for a squire's daughter, but he knew how to carry himself. The squire struck him hard across the face, and although he could have killed the old man with a blow, he never hit back. He had to let the girl go, and he let her go gracefully, like a gentleman. He loved her too, poor old chap, for he never married until quite late in life.'

The girl had been listening eagerly with something in her manner which made him feel that she had only been checking herself with an effort of will from interrupting with a dozen questions. When at last I made a long-enough pause she leant a little towards me, and asked in a queer strained voice: 'Tell me, please—was the girl a Miss Merryweather?'

A name I had heard my father mention leapt back into my memory across the years.

'By all that's wonderful,' I exclaimed, 'it was!'

'Then I know your grandfather's name—and yours, Mr Bishop.'

I stood up and stared at her.

'What are you telling me?' I said, hardly able to control my voice.

'You wouldn't know it. My name is Sergeant. But that Miss Merryweather afterwards became my great grandmother! You see, I too knew the story, but I didn't know it happened here.'

For a long moment we could only stare at one another. It was not the coincidence which baffled me, because I believed that what we call a coincidence is only the outward showing of something done in secret, and with a purpose, by Fate or Providence.

'That we should meet here!' I heard her say in a strange, sunken voice.

'Here of all places!'

'And in this very room!' I said.

She was looking about her dazedly as if in a trance.

'Yes, it was here,' she said in a low voice, but in the tone of one stating a simple fact. 'But the room was a little different then. The sideboard was behind me instead of over there.'

I looked. It may have been due to auto-suggestion, but I seemed to remember the great sideboard standing in the place she indicated.

'And we were sitting at the other end of the table with our backs to the window.'

She said We, and the word sounded hardly strange to me, for I, too, remembered— memories that glowed and vanished and glowed again like a failing lamp, giving me no more than glimpses of something which had happened, and yet never happened to me in this life.

'And that chair was still in the same place by the window, and your beaver hat was on it . . . and he came in . . . and you jumped up, overturning the chair on which you had been sitting . . . and I covered my face with my hands. She covered her face with her hands now, and began to rock herself to and fro as if in pain.

'It was with his whip that he struck you across the face ... it left a great red mark . . . Oh, John!'

John was my grandfather's name, but it happened not to be mine. And as she spoke I felt the smart of that whip, and touched my cheek gently with the tips of my fingers.

For the moment I was inarticulate. I knew no name to call her by. I was like a dumb man struggling for speech.

She stood up, all a-tremble, and suddenly lowered her hands from her face to grope for a wisp of a pocket handkerchief. I moved towards her. And a moment later she had slipped into my arms as if we were lovers long declared. Who shall say that we were not? In that moment I knew we were, and my heart melted for her as it beat against hers. I bent my face to hers, but she drew back suddenly with a little moan.

'No,' she cried, 'no! Oh, wait a little! Not yet!'

The strange experience which had overtaken us in a moment left us as suddenly, and left us dazed. We were just two strangers again, a man and a maid, chance-met at a country inn, who now stared sheepishly at one another. Her face flamed red, and once more she covered it with her hands. I saw her shoulders heave with sobs. She felt her way back to her place at the table and sat there silent, her face still covered, breathing spasmodically.

I stood and watched her. Then was not the time to theorise over what strange forces had been set at work by us two meeting in that old room. I preferred to think that it was willed so, that Destiny had used a slipping clutch and a man's curiosity to view the scene of an ancestor's romance, to bring together two people who had been planned to mate from the beginning of time.

'What do you think of me?' she asked suddenly in a low, tremulous voice. 'Was it madness? I've never . . . I've never . . .'

'My dear Miss Sergeant,' I said, gently, 'something very strange has happened to both of us. I think I know what it means, and so do you in your heart of hearts. We know each other so well now, although we never met—so far as we can be certain—until an hour ago. But we're not strangers, you and I.'

She rose unsteadily again, and turned towards the door.

'I can't speak to you now. I am going to my room. I—I can't think. I must try to understand.'

I let her go without a word, and I had no anxiety. It was as if my poor old grandfather were smiling and nodding reassurance to me across the worlds. I stood there smoking, trying hard to solve a problem which I may never solve, but with a mind unweighted and full of a new strange happiness.

I saw her next at the breakfast table. She had evidently schooled herself to meet me, and although neither of us had any doubt of what was in the other's mind, we made no allusion to those strange moments on the preceding night.

For twenty miles her way was the same as mine, and her car would be ready for her by midday. I said that I would wait with her until then and ride along with her.

'So we shall be fellow travellers for a little way,' she said, smiling.

But I knew, and she knew too, that we were destined to be fellow-travellers on a longer journey.